Baby
Girl II

Compilation and Introduction copyright © 2009 by
Vickie Stringer Publishing/Triple Crown Enterprises
PO Box 6888
Columbus, OH 43205
www.TripleCrownPublications.com

Library of Congress Control Number: 2009927424
ISBN 13: 978-0-9820996-7-4
Editor-in-Chief: Vickie M. Stringer
Assistant Editors: Maxine Thompson, Alana Boutin
Cover Design: Leap Graphics
Photography: Treagen Kier
Graphic Designer: Valerie
Model: Diamond
Hair: Diamond
Make up: Candace
Book Design: Brian Holscher

First Trade Paperback Edition Printing

10 9 8 7 6 5 4 3 2 1

Printed in the United States of America

Acknowledgments

First and foremost, I would like to thank God for my innumerable blessings. I thank Him for all that I am and for all that I am not.

To my mother, Brenda Moore who has loved and cared for me in the special way that only a mother can.

To my daddy, James "T-Pot" Moore, who always said that I would be a "paperback writer" someday. (smile)

To my grandmothers, Vera Moore and Essie Graves, thank you for your nurturing and guidance. I inherited my "old soul" from you.

To my aunt, Mary Ann Frazier, for all of her advice, strength, and never-ending support. To my aunts Brenda, Ethel, Algie, and Gloria, and to my uncles David Moore, Dwight Brooks, Charles Johnson, Dennis and Joseph Graves Jr., I love you!

To some of the best friends anyone could pray for: Marshell McCall, LaShanda Albert, Canvas Dotson, J.B. Mooney, Kimberly "Kay" Hills, and Joseph Ivy for reading my work, giving me feedback, and pushing me to pursue a future in writing. Thank you, "Aunt" Rhonda Fitzhugh for being there when my computer was "on the blink". Angela Hills, Antoinette Mays, Teri Johnson, Perry Byrd, Della Sain, Florida Jasper, and Keith Brooks...Love ya!

To Vickie Stringer and Triple Crown Publications for seeing potential in me and helping to bring it forth, I am truly grateful! To the best editors around, Maxine Thompson and Alanna Boutin, thank you!

Last, but certainly not least, to my younger relatives: Travis Moore, James "Jay" Moore, Alayla Williams, Ahmarri Farr, Corinthian Graves, and Ayanna Campbell. May you always remember that the sky is not the limit...there are no limits!

I love you all.

Dedication

This book is dedicated to all of the loved ones that I lost in recent years: My Granddaddy, Frank Moore, my cousin Tiffany Ann Brooks, and my aunt Bobbie Moore.

One

I should have known that my love for Shard Phaylon would drive me crazy one day.

It looked as if that day had finally arrived.

I *had* to be crazy. I mean, why the hell else would I be lying up in a hospital bed in Cancun, Mexico, with plastic tubes snaking from my nostrils while a doctor told my man that I had nearly succeeded in taking my own life a few hours earlier.

Granny would have a double heart attack if she knew what I tried to do to myself, I thought. *I'm a badass Brown woman. We Browns are supposed to be stronger and more resilient than the average chick.*

I had been raised, or better yet, *trained*, by my vivacious grandmother and my three gorgeous, gold-digging aunts. They had taught me how to capitalize on my most valuable assets: namely, my beautiful face and voluptuous body, in order to hook a man with status, power, and wealth. Somewhere along the road of adolescence, though, I had rejected their teachings and I had decided to let my heart call all of the shots. Just look what my heart had gotten me into, though.

"If Kyla would have swallowed just a couple more of those sleeping pills, she would have been a goner," I could hear the Hispanic male doctor telling Shard. "And that would have been a real tragedy considering the circumstances. Two lives would have been lost because of one foolish act."

Two lives? I thought. *What two lives?*

After the doctor had left the room, Shard slipped his hands into the pockets of his black Armani pants and strolled over to the large window in my second-floor room at Ameri-med Hospital. He stared out into the night, appearing to be in deep thought about something. I silently watched him.

It was amazing. Even after all of the drama and pain that I had been through in the past few hours, all I could focus on at that moment was his blinding beauty. Shard had that effect on the fairer sex. A girl could drown in those slanted, liquid eyes and take leave of her senses while she marveled at his smooth, honey-colored skin, sleek, ebony hair, chiseled cheekbones, and supple lips. God had made him naturally prettier than many women that I knew.

His gaze suddenly shifted from the window to me. When he saw that I had awakened again, he sauntered over and took a seat in the chair next to my bed. "You feeling any better?"

"Yeah, a little bit."

"You need anything?"

"I'm okay." I tried to sit up, but discovered that my head felt too heavy to lift. "So what all did the doctor say?"

Shard sniffed and shook his head. "Trust me, you don't even wanna know."

"Don't wanna know *what*?"

He took a deep breath. "Before we get into all that, I need you to answer a question for me." I anticipated the question before he even asked. He leaned forward and stared into my eyes. "Why did you do it?"

Because you drove me to it! I wanted to scream at him. *Maybe I wouldn't have tried to kill myself if you hadn't turned your back on me when I needed you!* I didn't give voice to my accusatory thoughts, though. Instead, I closed my eyes again and sighed heavily. "I couldn't keep living with what we did in New York, Shard. I'll never forgive myself for that. I just kept hearing Slide screaming in my ears. I tried to tell you that I couldn't handle it, but you acted like I was making shit up. I guess I finally reached my breaking point. I couldn't take it anymore."

Shard was a drug lord in our native St. Louis. He knew that I had been severely traumatized ever since I had assisted him in an armed robbery that his supplier had ordered a month earlier. Shard and I had traveled to New York to swipe one-hundred thousand dollars from a nightclub owner named Slide. Shard had asked me to seduce Slide and to get him alone and defenseless in a motel room while he had concealed himself in the bathroom, calculating the perfect opportunity to hold him up. He had promised me that we wouldn't harm Slide.

Shard had lied, though, because he didn't just take Slide's money that night.Shard had taken his life, too. He had fired three bullets into Slide's body and had simultaneously changed my life forever. The guilt that my contribution to the crime had brought upon me had slowly eaten away at my sanity. Shard had brought me to Cancun with his crew to try and take my mind off of my misery. The sandy beaches and aquamarine skies of Mexico had done little to restore my waning mental health, though, and in a last-ditch attempt at atonement for my sin, I had gone into the bathroom at our villa and swallowed a toxic dose of Zolpidem.

Shard seemed intent on avoiding any discussion about Slide or the incident in New York. He sat back in his chair. "If Mal hadn't gone back to the house and found you on the floor, you wouldn't even be talking to me right now. Do you know how serious that is, baby girl? You *overdosed*." When I didn't respond, he stood to his feet and paced the floor. "I had to tell these doctors that all of this was an accident, so when they ask you, make sure you stick to the story."

I nodded. "Okay."

Shard suddenly stopped pacing again and folded his arms. "So when were you planning to tell me that you stopped taking your birth control?"

I frowned at him. "What are you talking about? I didn't stop taking them."

"Yeah, well, the doctor and two nurses say otherwise," he spat. He stopped pacing and refocused on me. "Not only did you almost kill yourself, but you almost gave yourself an abortion, too."

My body went numb. "*Abortion*? What the hell are you talking about?"

His brow was now set in anger. "They're saying that you're pregnant."

I was so stunned that my ability to speak momentarily left me. "That's why I've been getting so sick lately," I finally stammered. "But … that can't be right. I may have missed a few of my birth control pills, but I didn't …"

"What do you mean, you '*missed a few*'?" Shard sneered at me. "Taking that birth control was *your* responsibility, Kyla, not mine. I completely trusted you with that. How could you let this shit happen?"

My eyes filled with tears. "I swear I didn't do it on purpose," I said truthfully. "You know how crazy and hectic things have been for us these past couple of months. My head has just been all over the place."

He took a couple of deep breaths and gradually calmed himself. "Well, fortunately, that's one problem that we can still solve. Let's just get it taken care of. There should be a couple of clinics in the city where you can have it fixed quick, right? You can probably go in and do it tomorrow."

"Yeah … probably. But …"

"But, what?"

"I don't know how I feel about abortions," I said. "I never really thought about it before, so how can I make a decision that big in just a couple of days?"

Shard reached out and took my chin in his hand. "No secrets, no lies," he prepped me as he always did. "Is this child mine?"

"How could you even ask me that, Shard?" I had only been with one other person before Shard, and had not been with anyone else since I had begun dating him over a year earlier.

"I'm sorry if that question seems harsh, but you have to understand my position. It's not like we're together every second of the day. I can't completely account for anybody's actions but my own. I trust you about as much as I can trust anybody. But if you betrayed me, I could never trust or love you again." He clutched my chin tighter and stared into my eyes. "So I'm going to ask you a second and final time: *Is this my child?*"

"Yes," I repeated without hesitation as I met his stare. He watched me for what seemed like the longest three seconds of my life. After a moment, though, I could see the reservations leave his face.

"It seems like you want to keep it," he finally said.

"No. Well ... maybe. But if you're gonna resent me, I won't."

He shook his head. "There's no way I'm taking the blame for this one, too. I'm leaving it all in your hands this time. I'll back you on whatever you decide."

By the time we arrived back in St. Louis two nights later, I had made a reluctant decision to keep the child. The fact that I was carrying Rashard Phaylon's firstborn was my only motivation to keep living. After all, I had wanted to share all that I could with Shard. I loved that man like I loved air. I had loved him from the moment I laid my eyes on him at the tender age of seventeen.

Even though I had known that he was six years my senior, I had to have him. Though I had been told that he was the heir to his incarcerated father's illegal drug throne, I had to have him. And even though everybody had warned me that he was too streetwise, too restless, and just too plain pretty to ever settle down and build a real life with me, I *had* to have him.

I'd always been a beautiful girl, and men were helplessly drawn to my café au lait skin, feline eyes, past shoulder-length black hair, and poisonous curves. Shard, however, was the only man I'd ever met who hadn't seemed the least bit interested in me. I had shamelessly thrown myself at him at every opportunity, only to have my monstrous ego slammed by his arrogance and indifference. It was only after months of relentlessly chasing him that I had melted his chilly veneer and finally burrowed my way into his heart.

Of course, I had to fight for Shard's love. *Literally.* Shard was originally from East St. Louis and had been heavily involved with a girl named Zaina there when our affair had begun. After learning of my relationship with him, Zaina had made it her sole mission to make me miserable. She had even violently attacked me on more than one occasion. It was only after Shard had taught me the importance of fighting back that I had realized just how strong I really was. Shard had hurt me in more ways than I had ever dreamed possible, but he had also taught me some of the most precious lessons about life that I had ever learned.

I knew that I had to call on the survival skills that he had passed on to me in order to put Slide's death behind me. So when we returned to our plush, two-story brick home in the suburb of Chesterfield, I slipped back into my old routine of cooking, cleaning, and catering to Shard like the "perfect" woman would.

Though we weren't married, I had always been content to play the role of housewife. Shard kept me laced with the finest in designer clothing and jewelry, so I figured that making his home comfortable for him was the least I could do. I had somehow convinced myself that I shouldn't be bothered by the fact that actually finding him *at* home was as rare as a UFO sighting. He had wandering eyes, and his feet seemed to follow those eyes wherever they roamed. Shard had an embarrassment of riches when it came to women. He loved me, but he couldn't seem to limit himself physically to just one woman. Shard needed to have options. I think he felt confined when he didn't.

The first week after our return from Cancun, he actually came home every single night. It was obvious that he was observing me just to assure that I wouldn't lock myself in a room and resort to drastic measures to solve my problems again. To distract myself from those issues, I tried to focus and prepare for the birth of my child, but I didn't feel extremely connected to the seed that was growing inside of me. The only kinship that I felt to it came through knowing that Shard had planted it there. There was a part of him existing, thriving, and developing within me, and I took pride in that fact.

Shard had never expressed a desire to be a father, and it soon became glaringly obvious to me that he didn't welcome the idea. He merely tried to get used to it. I would sit home all day, wondering how I would survive nine months without the kind of advice, empathy, and support that only a mother, grandmother, and aunts could give a woman who was in my condition for the very first time.

My momma, Camille, had left me in St. Louis with Granny when I was just a baby and had headed to Boston to enjoy life on her own terms. She and I communicated on occasion, but she had never been constant in my world, so I had been raised by my grandmother and the three Brown sisters who still lived in the city.

As fate would have it, though, I had not spoken to Granny or my aunts, Denise, Monica, and Jazz, in nearly a year's time. I had broken my ties with the women after I had discovered that Jazz had committed the definitive act of disloyalty.

She had slept with Shard.

Incredibly, the rest of my family had sided with Jazz, accusing me of being too "young and dumb" to understand that the proverbial blood was thicker than water. Angry, bitter, and full of unspeakable hurt, I had packed my bags and left the only home I had ever known. I had moved to Chesterfield with Shard and had vowed to never exchange another word with my conniving aunts or biased grandmother again.

My cousin, Nina, was two years older than I was, and she was also my best friend. Even though she was Denise's daughter, she and I had remained close throughout the inner-family feud. Nina and Camille were the only two members of the Brown family with whom I had maintained contact. I was sure that they had told the rest of the family that I was expecting, but everyone still kept their distance. We just couldn't move past the resentment that separated us.

As time wore on, I began to grow worried that my relatives had not emotionally equipped me for motherhood. I knew that I was too frivolous, selfish, and needy to have a child. As much as I had tried to buck the system that the Browns had established, I realized that in many ways, I was still just like my self-centered family members.

In addition to worrying about the future, I was still secretly depressed about my past. In spite of my tireless effort to forget, I was being revisited daily by memories of the incident in New York. I felt like *I* had pulled the trigger. Shard's dangerous lifestyle had never bothered me before; but as time went on, I learned to hate the drug game and everything that it required of its participants.

For the first time since I had begun dating Shard, it became blatantly obvious to me that the cons of his lifestyle far outweighed the pros. Shard's business had nearly cost me my mind and my life, too. I could only hope that it wouldn't eventually ask me to pay an even higher price.

Two

My first trimester was hell.

My days were ruled by morning sickness, body aches, and severe mood swings. I grew tired of staying alone, so even though I was pregnant, I started running the streets with Shard again. In fact, I began to cling to him tighter than ever before. I didn't want him to force me to stay home, so I hid all of my discomfort from him. When I had to throw up, I would go into the bathroom, close the door, and flush the toilet so that it would drown out the sound of my retching. I even stopped wearing my trademark revealing clothing. Instead, I opted for loose blouses tied at the waist, which I paired with wide-legged pants or flowing skirts and dresses to hide my changing figure. I still managed to look sexy, and for the first few months, with my clothes on, it was impossible to tell that I was carrying a child. As long as I didn't *look* pregnant yet, I figured nobody would go out of their way to treat me like I was.

And nobody did—not even Shard. Everything that he and I did was at the same level that it had been before. The clubbing, the partying, and the sex. For the most part, we didn't debate about baby names or make big plans for the birth. In fact, Shard never even seemed to take the time to contemplate parenthood.

There were nights when I would lie in bed and wonder if I had made the right decision by keeping the child. I began to see just how lightly Shard was taking his new fatherhood role when the call of the hustle started proving more powerful than the call of the home life.

I was well into my fourth month of pregnancy when his supplier, Eli, the same Eli who had conceived of Slide's robbery, had presented Shard with another big-money scheme.

Shard's father had gone into business with Eli several years ago, back when Mr. Phaylon had first founded his booming drug cartel. Mr. Phaylon had pulled his two oldest sons into the game with him, but had kept his youngest and favorite, Shard, out of the life of crime. It was only after Shard's father and both of his brothers had gotten busted and had been given lengthy prison sentences that Shard had taken over the empire. He had brought his best friend, Mal, and two other partners, Shorty and Hutch, into the venture as well. And even after seven years, Shard was still working closely with Eli.

I was sitting next to Shard on the bed, polishing my toenails, when he got Eli's call. He was lying back, staring at a basketball game. When his cell phone started chiming, he sighed and reached over to grab it.

"What's up?" he said into the receiver. He was silent as he listened to the other party speak. "Word?" he uttered with sudden interest. "When? Ah-ight, well, just hit me back with the details ... Ah-ight."

He ended his call and placed the phone back on the nightstand. "Eli's keeping the business coming," he declared as he reclined back again.

"Really?" Eli's name only served as a reminder of the night in New York. I didn't want to speak about him. I didn't even want to think about him.

"Yeah," Shard replied. "We're going into this three-way deal with one of Eli's connects. The payoff's gonna be ridiculous, too. Just the type of lick I been waiting on."

I didn't respond. I continued to run the small brush in even, parallel strokes over my nail.

"Eli's real cool with this nigga from Chicago," continued Shard. "Dude is here in St. Louis now. Eli put him down with me. He wants a quick look at my product."

I finally looked up at him with a raised eyebrow. "Is this gonna be anything like what y'all did to ... Slide?" The sound of *that* name was even worse than the sound of Eli's. It had taken everything inside of me just to speak it.

Shard shook his head. "It's nothing like that. It's strictly a money deal. It won't be anything foul. Trust me. I've been doing deals like this since I was eighteen."

I was skeptical. "I don't think you should do it."

"Why not? You're always down for shit like this."

Though he was considered underworld royalty, Shard loved to get his hands dirty as if he were a minion. He was suave and could be sophisticated when he wanted, but he seemed to get a real thrill out of pulling heists and shooting off rounds. Most guys in the game behaved like gangsters, but Shard was more like a *mobster.* He was the only man I knew who wore diamond cuff links and Versace sunglasses, even when he was about to jack a fool. He was the only man I knew from the 'hood who knew which vintage wine perfectly complemented a meal. He was the only man I'd ever met who knew that metal spoons tainted the taste of caviar, and that you never had *real* spaghetti until you'd eaten it at a bistro in the heart of Florence, Italy.

His looks and his charm often prevented people from understanding just how lethal he really was. I had often wondered if he enjoyed getting involved in the schemes just so that he could prove his fearlessness.

I shrugged. "I don't know, Shard. I just keep thinking about—"

"About what happened in New York?" he interrupted with an exasperated sigh. Instead of responding, I just leaned over as far as my bulging little belly would allow and began to blow my wet nails.

"I don't want to talk about New York anymore, Kyla. It's counterproductive for us to keep going there in conversation. It's not solving or changing anything. You know that, right?" Shard was not making eye contact with me. As he spoke, he stared at the television screen.

"It doesn't bother you, though?" I screwed the cap back on the bottle of polish. "You're completely okay with the way things went down that night? It hasn't stayed on your mind for the past couple of months?"

"No." He finally turned to look at me. "You gotta take control of your emotions. You can't let them handle you like that. You sit around here and let that shit run through your head all day, every day, and it's gonna drive you crazy for real this time. Everything that went down that night was all on me. *Everything*. You understand?" I slowly nodded my head.

"Ah-ight then. Just drop it, okay?"

"Okay." I scooted over the mattress until I had bridged the gap between us. Then, I rested my head on his shoulder. He welcomed me by wrapping his arm around me.

"I need to tell you something, baby girl, but I don't want you to start flipping out about it. The only reason that I'm even telling you is because I want you to know what's up in case you hear anything from anybody. No secrets, no lies, right?"

His words were starting to make me nervous. I sat up and looked at him, waiting for him to continue.

"I think that the Feds are on my ass. Some niggas in East and a couple of people from U City who scored from me have told me that a couple of Fed agents have been asking them questions. A dude stopped Mal day before yesterday and started asking him some shit, too. Have you noticed the white van parked by the school down the block sometimes when you leave?"

"No. I never paid any attention before."

"I think it's some surveillance. But it's nothing to worry about. I've been investigated before. They couldn't bring charges up on me because they said all the evidence was circumstantial."

He was so calm. How could he be? I was shivering like I was standing in a blizzard.

"That sounds serious," I said. "Federal agents? What are they trying to do? Why are they even investigating you? They must have a reason—"

Shard interrupted me. "Don't start panicking, ah-ight? Everything's under control. Somebody probably tipped them off, so they have to follow through with the leads that they get. It's just their procedure, but trust me, it'll all die down."

"Are you sure it's nothing to worry about?"

"Nothing for *you* to worry about anyway." He held me tighter, and instantly, I felt safe and secure. I wanted to believe anything that he said to me. If he told me that there was no cause to fret, then I wouldn't fret.

I was surprised when Shard's hand moved slowly over my torso and settled on my stomach. I looked down at my round little belly. "It feels funny, huh?"

"Yeah. The skin is tight. Is it uncomfortable?"

"No, it's all right." His palm moved over my belly in a circular motion. It was very soothing. Suddenly, I felt a jerk inside of my abdomen.

"*Oh*," I squealed, sitting up straighter. "What was that?" I placed a hand over Shard's and looked up at him with a frown. "Did you feel that?"

His eyes gleamed with fascination. "Hold up. Be still."

He pressed his hand more firmly into my skin. The jerky movements jolted lightly through my midsection again. "Oh, shit, I think the baby's kicking." I watched as he rolled my T-shirt up and placed his ear against my belly. He chuckled softly. "That's crazy. This kid is no joke. It's like football season in there or something. The kicks are something serious."

I laughed softly as I put my hand on his head and rubbed his hair, watching him as he continued to listen. Suddenly, I felt warm and tingly all over. It was a very surreal experience. It was the first time that we had ever really discussed the unborn child since I had found out that I was pregnant. I was surprised by how nice the moment felt. Shard seemed to be reading my mind as he rubbed my belly again.

"This is wild, right?" he asked. "Thinking of yourself as somebody's mother?"

"Yeah, and you as somebody's daddy. What could be wilder than that?"

"You think it'll be a boy or a girl?" I gazed down at the now-calm bulge.

"I don't know. Can the doctor determine the sex yet?"

"Yeah. He offered to tell me the last time I was there, but I didn't really want to know. Maybe it'll be a girl."

"So you want a girl?"

"Maybe. Don't you think we'd have a pretty daughter?"

"Yeah." He smiled softly as he pinched my chin. "She would probably look like you. That's every dude's nightmare, though—having a cute daughter."

"Why is that?"

"Because every man knows how *he* reacts to a pretty woman. He knows how dudes think. He doesn't want anybody thinking those things about his little girl. And he *definitely* doesn't want anybody trying to *do* that freaky shit with her."

I tossed my head back and laughed. "Oh—like all of the things that you've done with me?"

"*Exactly,*" he admitted, surprising me. "I wouldn't want to think about some little punk going there with my child. I would flip out. My daughter would have to stay innocent forever."

"Men are such a hypocrites." I shook my head. "Y'all want your women to be freaks in the bedroom, but you don't want your daughters to be that same freak for *her* man."

"*Hell,* nah. That's out of the question." He watched my belly a while longer before he spoke again. "Nah, but for real, though, I been thinking a lot more seriously lately. Way more than I usually do."

"About what?"

He shrugged his shoulders. "Just about myself. My life." He leaned his head back and gazed up at the ceiling. "You know what's crazy? I'm damn near twenty-six years old, and I still don't know why I'm here. I don't know what my purpose is. I don't know the reason I'm here on this earth, occupying this particular space in time. There's gotta be a reason that each of us is here. There's gotta be a reason why we as human beings are higher than the animals. We're able to rationalize and meditate. That must mean that every human life has a purpose. I just don't know what mine is, though."

"My granny used to tell me that everybody lives just so that they can die," I said. "Death is the greatest event of life."

"See, that's what I mean. If dying is so important, then the way that we live must be just as important, right? There's *gotta* be a connection. If there isn't, then the whole concept of life makes no sense."

"Maybe life isn't supposed to make sense," I said. "Maybe we spend too much time trying to figure it out. That's when we defeat the whole purpose of living. Great thinkers and philosophers have been trying to answer these questions since the beginning of time. If nobody's come up with an answer yet ... then maybe there just isn't one."

Shard shook his head. "I don't buy that. I ain't trying to answer no million-year-old question here. The question I'm trying to answer is only twenty-five. What's *my* purpose? That's all I want to know." He started rubbing my belly again.

I nodded. "So ... do you believe in Heaven and Hell?" I asked. We had never really discussed religion.

"I believe in Heaven. I told you that my mother died when I was just a lil' one. It really threw me for a loop because she was the picture of health, y'know? She was young and happy. And she was beautiful—the most beautiful woman I had ever seen. I was closer to her than my brothers were. They were some hardheads. They wanted to run the streets at a real young age, but me, I just preferred to stay near my mother. I was the youngest, so when she got sick, everybody tried to protect me by not telling me how serious it was. I was thinking that she had something common like the flu. She lay in bed for about a month, dying, and I didn't even know it.

"I would run home from school to go and jump onto her bed and tell her everything that I had done that day. It was like she had lay there all day, just waiting for me. She loved me more than anybody has ever loved me. But one day I came home ... and her bed was empty. She was gone." He sighed and shook his head.

"Anyway," he continued, "everybody told me that she was gone to Heaven. That was the only explanation they ever gave me. She had gone to Heaven so that she could rest better. Ever since then, I've had this mental picture of Heaven as a perfect place. I believe that my mother is still young there. I think she's still happy and still beautiful. I have to believe that Heaven is real. Otherwise, I can't believe that she's okay."

As I listened to him, my eyes were brimming with warm tears. "So if you believe there's a Heaven, you must believe there's a God," I said.

"I don't know. Do you?"

"Sometimes," I said as the tears belatedly spilled over my lids. "Sometimes I don't, but sometimes I really do. The times when I do believe Somebody's up there watching me, those are the times when I really worry. It worries me because I'm afraid of what He might see." Shard didn't respond. "If there is Somebody up there," I added, "do you ever worry about how He'll judge you for the life that you live?"

"No. I don't think He'll judge me any harsher than He would you for turning a blind eye to the way that I live. If God is real, then I expect Him to judge me. But if He's as just and fair as they say He is, then I don't expect to be judged any harsher than you or anybody else."

I nodded and laid my head on his shoulder again. We sat in silence, both apparently surprised by the spiritual tone our conversation had taken. Long after Shard had fallen asleep, I still lay there thinking about it all.

The next morning, I awoke and rested in bed, savoring the early silence for a few moments. Then I sat up and eased off the mattress to keep from waking Shard. I made my way to the bathroom and took a long shower. After stepping out of the tub, I wiped the steam from the mirror and stared at my reflection. I gazed in wonder at my naked body, almost five months full with child. It was beautiful. Then I tenderly rubbed shea butter all over my belly. Once I was dressed, I went downstairs to the kitchen.

I had a strong craving for pancakes. As I moved around the room, stooping and bending to remove the mixing bowl and electric griddle from the cabinet, I felt the jerking that I had felt in bed the night before. I smiled as I looked down at my belly. I didn't know where my sudden sense of closeness to the fetus inside of me had come from. I was pretty sure that those kicks had started it all, though. Those kicks had made Shard and me realize that there was more than just a seed that had been fertilized inside of me. There was a person there. A person that shared our flesh and blood. I was beginning to feel the connection.

In his own way, I believed that Shard had begun to feel it as well. I was standing over the griddle, turning the golden brown pancakes when I felt him ease up behind me and slide his arms around my waist.

His hands caressed my belly. "Good morning."

"'Morning. Are you hungry?"

"Nah. I'm gonna leave that to you. You know I don't eat heavy in the morning." He walked over to the stainless steel refrigerator and removed the bottle of orange juice. I watched as he produced two glasses from the cabinet and filled each one. It was nice to spend the early morning with him. It was such a rare occurrence. I was just about to tell him how good I felt that morning when he said, "Guess what?"

"What?"

"I just got off the phone with ole boy that Eli put me down with. Looks like we're definitely going through with this deal. This shit is going down in a major way."

My smile faded. The plastic spatula in my hand paused in midair. "So ... you're going to do it? You're doing business with him again?"

"Yeah."

"I *really* don't think you should." I shook my head, making my ponytail whip from side to side. "I don't want you to. Eli told us that the cops called off the investigation on Slide's murder. Y'all got away with that, so why do you keep gambling with our future?"

"Because I need to do this, Kyla. This is big. This is gonna buy a whole helluva lot of diapers and milk for that baby."

"We're not hurting for money. Don't use the baby as an excuse to do some dirty work that you were already gonna do anyway."

"So what you want from me, then? You want me to tell Eli that I'm not down with it? Do you know how many favors he's done for my family over the years? He's pulled all kinds of strings for us. When my ole man got locked up, he asked me to look out for Eli. Every time I go to visit him, the first thing he asks is if I'm taking care of Eli."

"It's cool that you're taking care of him. But is *he* taking care of *you*?" There. I had finally said it. I had finally asked the question that had been lingering in my mind ever since the first time that I had heard Eli's name.

"What? You've seen the paper that he's has dropped off in my lap. How else you think I'm able to keep shit moving so hard around here? How else you think I'm able to lace you the way that I do? I gotta put in work for the money. Nobody's gonna give me a damn thing for free, ah-ight?"

"But I'm not talking about the money. I'm not even talking about Eli anymore. This is bigger than all of that. This is about you, Shard. This is about me, and this baby." I pointed at my belly. "What about last night? The way we were talking ... It was like we finally decided that we really *do* want this child. I thought we bonded with it last night. I thought we bonded with each other."

He shrugged his shoulders. "I guess we did. But what has that got to do with this?"

"Everything. You're gonna keep involving yourself in shit like this, knowing that you're about to be a father? You're cool with that?"

"*My* daddy was doing this years before I was even born,"

he pointed out.

"Yeah, and look where your daddy is now. Was he such a good example for his kids? Both your brothers are in jail. And now you're doing the same thing that ruined them. So evidently, your daddy wasn't the greatest—"

"Ay, don't talk about my father, ah-ight?" he hissed vehemently. I was startled into silence. "There wasn't anything he wouldn't have done for me or my brothers. You don't know what we went through. You don't know shit about my family, so don't talk about them."

"I know I got your family right here inside of me. I got somebody inside of me who's gonna be a bigger part of you than your father, or your brothers, or that punk-ass Eli could *ever* be. Why don't you prioritize, Shard? What's most important to you?"

"Right now, the most important thing is taking care of this business."

I shook my head. "All you wanna do is hustle. And here I am, with my silly ass, thinking that things were gonna be different after the way we talked last night. I thought that we both saw something better for the future. I really believed that you were examining your way of life."

"I'm constantly examining my way of life. Last night I just felt like sharing my thoughts with you. That didn't mean that I was about to quit the game or run down to the river to get baptized. Don't stress me about this, Kyla. The thing that I love most about you is the way that you respect what I do. You've never complained about the way that I live, and you've never tried to change me. Don't try to change me now. This is who I am."

When I didn't respond, he placed both hands on my shoulders and squeezed. "So what ... you don't love me no more?" he asked, half-joking. "I can't get no love from you?"

I closed my eyes, wishing that I could express the sudden worry and fear that had descended upon me seemingly overnight. "You know I love you." I wrapped my arms around his neck. "I love you so much, it hurts sometimes. That's why I only want the best for you. I want the best for *us*."

"I do, too." He placed a firm kiss on my lips. "But I got so much that I need to do. Paying off all my daddy's debt was only the first step. I did that for him, though; and now, I can focus more on the things that need to be done for me." He touched my chin. "And for you. I can't quit now. The only way that I could quit at this point was if my back was against the wall."

He released his hold on me and walked away. I knew that signified the end of the discussion. Shard was in the game to stay; and apparently, there was nothing I could do about it.

◊ ◊ ◊ ◊

That month, I turned twenty, and a couple of months later, Shard was twenty-six. I was emotionally spiraling out of control again. On most days, I didn't even have the energy to sit up in bed. Shard even noticed my state, so he left me with a big chunk of cash to do some shopping. He didn't seem to realize that money and *things* no longer excited me or made me happy the way they had when we had first met. The walls had started closing in on me, though, so I forced myself out of the house and to the mall anyway.

Once I arrived there, I barely had the energy to function. I walked slowly down the corridor, gazing in the windows of all of the stores. I stopped in at Modish, one of my favorite boutiques. Inside, I wistfully ran my fingers over the beautiful pieces there—the silk halter tops, the body-hugging catsuits, the tight-fitting cashmere sweaters ... These were all things that I could no longer wear because of the dramatic change in my figure. I started wondering if I would be blessed with my flat stomach, tiny waist, and curvaceous hips and backside again once I gave birth. I decided then and there that if I didn't get my old body back, me and that child I was carrying were going to have some serious issues between us.

On the way out of the mall, I stopped at The Pretzel Shoppe and ordered a large, soft pretzel dipped in melted butter and rolled in thick, coarse salt. I ate quickly and was popping the last chewy morsel into my mouth when I stepped out to the parking lot. As I walked up to my car, I noticed the driver's-side door of the black Ford Taurus parked in the adjacent space swing open. A tall, medium-brown, middle-aged black man stepped out. He was dressed in a black trench coat over a charcoal gray suit and a black necktie. He nodded a greeting at me. I ignored him as I popped the locks to the BMW. As I reached for the door handle, the reflection in the glass of my driver's-side window made me jump. I whirled around to see the strange man standing right behind me.

"I'm sorry," he said through his broom-thick mustache. "I didn't mean to startle you." He reached into his jacket pocket and produced a black leather wallet. Flipping open the flap, he showed me the silver shield that had been pinned there. "My name is Gregory Lewis. I'm an agent with the Federal Bureau of Investigation. I was wondering if I might ask you a few questions."

"What questions?"

"Are you Kyla Brown?"

"Yeah." I placed a hand on my hip. "Why you wanna know?"

Agent Lewis ignored my question.

"Are you acquainted with a Malcolm Hassan Richmond?" He returned the shield to his pocket and removed a mechanical pen and a small notepad.

"Yeah. I know Mal. Why?"

"What about a Terry 'Hutch' Webster, and a Mitchell 'Shorty' Templeton?"

"Yeah. I know 'em all. What's the purpose of all this?"

"The Bureau is conducting a special investigation in East St. Louis and all surrounding areas. We're following up on a few leads that we were given." Agent Lewis gazed down at his pad. "May I ask the nature of your relationship with these three individuals?"

"Um, I've known them for a little more than two years. I guess you could call them friends of mine."

"Friends? How did you meet? Did you meet them through Rashard Phaylon?"

I swallowed hard and leaned back against my car. "And how do you know that I'm acquainted with Rashard Phaylon?

You never asked me about him."

"I didn't have to. I already know about your involvement with him." He referred to his notepad. "You have been dating Rashard for approximately twenty-eight months. You've resided at his home at 1198 Tempest Drive in Chesterfield, Missouri, for approximately fourteen months." He looked at me again with raised eyebrows. "Correct?"

I wondered if he heard the tremble in my voice when I replied, "Correct."

"Are you familiar with one Eli Broadnax?"

"Nope." I crumpled up the wax paper that had held my pretzel.

"Excuse me?" Lewis gave me a surprised frown. "You *don't* know Eli Broadnax?"

"Nope. Never heard of him." I opened the car door. "So if that's all you need—"

"Just one more question." Lewis held his hand up. He peered at me intently through beady black eyes. "Have you ever traveled to the East Coast?"

I struggled to maintain my composure. "I've been to Boston. That's where my mother lives. Since you've done so much research on me, you should know that already, *Detective.*" I pointed at my belly. "It's freezing out here; and as you can see, I'm in no condition to be battling Mother Nature. So are we done?"

Lewis nodded vigorously. "Yeah." He took two steps back. "Of course." He watched as I climbed into the car, started the ignition, and backed out of my space. As soon as I was on the interstate, I flipped my cell phone open and called Shard.

He answered on the first ring. "What's up?"

"Hey, where you at?"

"On my way to U City. Why? You need something?"

"No. Guess who just came up to me at the mall?"

"Who?"

"Some guy with the FBI. He knew my name and every-thing. He—"

"Meet me at the Shell station at the corner on Broward," Shard interrupted. Before I could say another word, he hung up. In ten minutes' time, I was parking on the side of the small brick building on Broward Avenue. Shard's Rover was already waiting there. As soon as I parked, he climbed out and then walked over and got into the passenger seat of the BMW.

"Never talk to me about the business over the phone," he warned. I nodded.

"Now, what did the Fed say to you?"

"Like I said, he knew my name and everything. He was asking me about Mal, Hutch, Shorty, and Eli. He wanted to know if I knew them, and how I met them. He didn't ask me any spe-cific questions about you, though."

Shard was calm. "Yeah. He knew that me and you are together. He probably figured that he would have more luck get-ting information about *them* out of you. So what you tell him?"

"Not much. I swore that I had never heard of Eli. I knew I couldn't lie about knowing Mal and them, though, because we all live in the same city. He would have caught me in that one."

"Yeah. That's good. That's perfect. Look, if anybody else

comes up to you, you just stick with that. Whatever you do, don't ever mention Eli, ah-ight?"

"All right."

I knew that wouldn't be hard. I wanted to forget that I had ever known Eli anyway.

A couple of weeks passed, and there was no further mention of the FBI. I allowed myself the luxury of feeling slightly comfortable once more. I threw myself into a domestic role again, constantly cooking and cleaning, even when I was the only one in the house to enjoy the food and the tidy atmosphere. Shard would usually stay away all weekend and then return home on Monday, only to leave out again on Thursday. He kept an apartment on the east side, and he frequently had business out of town, so I fooled myself into believing that he wasn't staying away from me by *choice*. He had always been the best at not getting caught with other women when he didn't *want* to be caught.

I didn't know if he had begun to get careless, or if he just no longer cared if I found out about his infidelities. Whichever it was, the evidence I found one day as I was doing his laundry was so damning that I could no longer act oblivious: a tawny-colored makeup stain and a smudge of gold lipstick on his white Ralph Lauren shirt collar. I didn't even ask him for answers. I knew that he spent most of his Saturdays at a club called Icy with his crew. That had always been their favorite spot to relax. That Saturday I had called Shard, but he hadn't answered his phone. When I glanced at the clock on the wall, I saw that it was eleven fifty-seven pm. I dialed him again, and again, I got no answer. I even tried messaging him, to no avail.

Determined to get some answers, I grabbed my keys and waddled out of the house in my thin, baby doll-style maternity dress and coat. My hair was pulled into two ponytails, one on each side of my head hanging over my shoulders. I looked like a nine-year-old with a rubber ball stuck underneath her dress.

I drove all the way across town with the sole purpose of finding Shard and demanding that he come home immediately. When I finally arrived at Icy, I found the parking lot packed, nearly filled to capacity. I had to pull into a tight space at the edge of the lot and walk all the way up front. I was getting all kinds of strange stares as I marched right up to the front of the line, thrust my cover charge at the bouncer, and tottered through the metal detector.

The music inside of the club assaulted my ears. The crowds annoyed me. The heat irritated me. I wasn't even sure if he was there. I was being driven by pure instinct. I made my way over to the table that the crew usually occupied. Just as I had suspected, Mal and Hutch were sitting there. They were nursing drinks and conversing with two guys that I had never met before. I walked right up to the table. The loud, animated conversation came to a screeching halt as everyone looked up at me.

Mal jumped in my path, "Kyla ...," he started.

"What you doing here?" Hutch finished for him.

All eyes were on me.

I opted not to answer. "Where's Shard?"

Mal and Hutch exchanged a quick glance before Mal said, "Uh, he was here somewhere." He looked around with squinted eyes. "I don't know where he disappeared to, though."

I bit my bottom lip and turned slowly, scanning the crowd with my eyes.

"Kyla, I don't think it's real good for you to be here," said Mal. "It's hot. It's crowded, and it's smoky. That can't be good for the baby." He moved from the table. "Come on," he added, "let me walk you back out to the parking lot." He gently caught my arm at the elbow. Mal had always been extremely overprotective of me. He was Shard's best friend, but he had become like an older brother or a young uncle to me.

"No," I pulled back. "I need to see Shard. He's not answering his phone. I want him to come home with me." I gingerly touched my belly. "I don't feel good. I don't want to be by myself for the rest of the night."

Mal nodded. "I understand, baby girl." He guided me toward the exit by my shoulders. "As soon as I see him, I'll tell him to come home to you, okay?"

"Stop patronizing me, Mal." I pulled away again. "I want him *now.*"

I started back toward the table, throwing a fleeting glance at the dance floor. That was when I spotted Shard. He was leaning against the wall, nursing a bottle of champagne while a light brown-skinned girl danced on him like a stripper on a pole. She had long hair, long legs, and long slender hands, which she was using to rub his shoulders as she grinded on him.

I stood there, shocked, as I watched her row her solid body into his chest on down his lap. At first, I thought she was speaking intimately into his ear; but as I stared harder, I saw that she was softly nibbling on his earlobe. I watched as the tip of her tongue slid over his neck, up his chin, and then disappeared between his slightly parted lips. They began to kiss like lovers.

"Kyla," pleaded Mal, as he caught up to me. "Don't wig out now. You're pregnant." I ignored him and stalked out onto the dance floor, pushing people out of my way as I did.

"Kyla!" I heard Mal calling. He sounded far away by then, his voice drowned out by the music and the distance that I had put between us. I marched up to Shard and reached out to pry him from the girl. He looked up with a frown.

"What you think you doing?" I screamed at him. "Who is *she*?" I looked at the girl, who had taken several steps backwards.

Shard glanced at her, and then at me again. "That's a friend. That's all."

"Oh, *that's* all I am?" She placed her hands on her hips and gazed at him in disbelief. She looked at me and extended her hand. "How you doing? I'm Raven. And you're Kyla, right?"

I just sneered at her, then rolled my eyes and refocused my attention on Shard. "So what's up with this? You're standing up here having foreplay with this ho for the whole world to see?"

Raven looked stunned. "Wait a minute. Who you calling a ho? You don't even know me, girl. You betta watch who you're throwing them words at."

"Don't say a damn thing to her," Shard warned Raven. "Let me handle this." He then looked at me. "I know how it must have looked, but I only kissed her. That's all."

"Shard, you know that it's more than that," protested Raven. "We came here together, and we're leaving together. Why won't you just tell her?"

"I thought I told you to shut the hell up," he repeated, this time with more intensity. She looked upset, but she clamped her lips together anyway. Shard caught me by the arm and started to guide me off the dance floor. I allowed him to lead me out of the club exit and out to the cold parking lot. Then I turned to him, watching him expectantly and waiting for an explanation. Unshed tears stood in my eyes.

Shard sighed as he leaned back against a parked car in the lot and stared at me. "Why did you come down here?" he finally asked.

"Because ..." My voice was shaky. "I wanted you to come home with me." I blinked, and the tears glided down my face. "You're *never* there anymore. You're always claiming that you got 'business' to take care of." I waved toward the club. "So is *she* the business?"

"I came out here to kick it with my boys." His dark eyes were unreadable. Why had I never seen guilt, worry, or deceit in them? For the first time, I realized that his mystique wasn't always such a good quality.

"But she just said that y'all came here together," I interrupted. "No secrets, no lies. Did you come here with her or not?"

"Yeah," Shard finally confessed.

I groaned in pained frustration. "Every time I turn my back, you're doing this to me." I hissed through gritted teeth. I folded my arms over my chest and stared at him. "How many more are there? I see the way they all throw themselves at you. So how many have you been with since you met me?"

He chewed the inside of his cheek, then began to pop his knuckles with his hand. "I never brought anything in your face. No bitch has called the house or approached you with drama since Zaina. It never affected you in any way. Why do you wanna ask questions like this now? Don't rock the boat. You know you can't handle it."

My nostrils flared angrily, and the tears were still flowing. "You let me decide what I can and can't handle. I don't need you to try to protect my feelings, okay? Just tell me, who else have you screwed since you been with me? Tell me how many women."

"I don't know."

"You don't *know*? Has it been *that* many?"

"Yeah, Kyla! It's been *that* many, ah-ight? Why you acting all surprised about it? You said that you could handle it, didn't you?"

"So give me a number. Give me an estimate. Has it been more than five? More than ten?"

"I just told you that I don't know how many. I honestly don't. It's not like I keep records or nothing."

"But it has been more than ten, hasn't it?"

He slowly nodded his head. "Yeah," he admitted. "I guess it has."

I swayed unsteadily on my feet. It didn't seem real. How had he managed to sleep with all those women without me ever finding out? I didn't know what to say. I just turned and walked away from him. For once, Shard didn't chase me down or plead his case with me. Shit, he didn't have a case to plead this time.

All he could do was watch me leave.

The drive home was miserable. I cried so hard, I could barely see the road ahead of me. My hands were trembling, making it nearly impossible to hold the steering wheel steady. I didn't know how I was supposed to handle this situation. How was I supposed to respond to it? To discover that he had had sex with my aunt once had been confusing and humiliating. To find him at his apartment in East with that other girl had been infuriating. But this ... how was I supposed to deal with this?

When I arrived home and pulled into the garage, but I didn't get out immediately. Instead, I sat in the car, just gazing into space while the tears streamed incessantly down my face.

I'm not sure how long I sat there, but I eventually mustered enough strength to pull myself out of the driver's seat and into the house. Once inside, I paced back and forth across the kitchen floor, not knowing whether I should retreat upstairs to pack my clothes or just jump back into the car and speed away with nothing more than my dignity.

My sadness gave way to anger as I thought again about the number of women Shard had been with since he and I had been together. I had suspected two. Possibly even three. But *ten* or more? How could I have been so blind? Or maybe it hadn't been blindness, but mere stupidity.

I stomped out of the kitchen, through the dining room, and up the stairs. When I got into the master bedroom, I flung open the double doors of my closet. As I stared inside though, something happened to me. It was almost like a vision. I stared into the darkness of that closet, and it almost seemed that I was staring into a future without Shard. My future if I decided to walk away from him. I realized then that I didn't have the courage to leave him. I didn't have the heart. I didn't even have the desire. Suddenly, all of my negative energy shifted. I didn't want to lose him to that girl at the club. I didn't want to lose him to anyone. I made up my mind that I wouldn't. I determinedly swiped the tears from my face, then I rose to my feet and marched back downstairs. I headed back into the kitchen, where I rescued a large butcher's knife from the cutlery board on the countertop. Quickly, I grabbed my keys and stormed out of the back door.

I don't remember what thoughts were swirling through my head as I sped onto the interstate in the direction of the club again. All of the emotions that I felt as a result of what I had discovered were on the verge of brimming over and spilling out of me. The concentrated rage was practically humming in my ears.

I glanced at the digital clock on the instrument panel of the car as I pulled into the parking lot at Icy again. It was already two forty-five am. The club closed at three. Several vehicles had vacated the lot, leaving spaces empty. I circled the parking lot until I spotted Shard's Range Rover in the center aisle, then I looked for the nearest empty space. It was one row over and three spaces down. I parked there, cut the headlights, and killed the ignition.

My hands gripped the steering wheel so tightly, my knuckles had turned white. I watched as people drifted out of the club and headed to their respective vehicles. Some came out alone. Others came out as couples or in groups of threes and fours. I leaned forward and squinted when I saw Hutch emerge from the interior with some anonymous female hanging on his arm. Seconds later, Mal headed out. He was busy tying his white do-rag onto his head. He turned around and started to speak to someone in the shadows behind him.

That was when Shard appeared with Raven. I reached across the car and grabbed the knife from the seat next to me. Then, I pushed the door open and stepped out. I felt the cold air whip through my clothes as I waddled across the asphalt, clutching the handle of the knife as I approached the group.

"Yeah, man. So I guess we'll go and take care of that tomorrow then," I heard Mal telling Shard as they slapped each other a brotherly handshake.

"Bye, Mal," Raven called with a wave.

"Ah-ight, Ma. See you later."

I clenched my teeth together as I wielded the knife tighter in my hand and stalked right up to Shard and Raven. Shard looked at me and frowned. "Kyla?" The look in his eyes displayed his uncertainty of my intentions. I didn't respond to him. Instead, I zoned in on Raven. Her eyes grew wide with shock and fear as I raised the knife high above my head.

"Ay, what the hell you doing?" Shard yelled at me as the shiny blade glinted in the streetlight overhead. I saw him reach out to intercept my arm.

I let out a scream of rage as I attempted to sink the blade into Raven's flesh. I didn't even know where I was aiming. I didn't care. I just wanted to hurt her. I wanted her to feel the pain that I was feeling at that moment. I closed my eyes at the exact second that the blade should have struck her. I heard her scream as the serrated edge of the knife raked across firm flesh and muscle.

I opened my eyes in time to feel a pair of hands grab me and pull me back.

"Kyla!" cried Mal. He began to wrench the knife out of my shaking hand. "Drop it!" He twisted my wrist roughly until I had no choice but to release the weapon, sending it clattering noisily to the concrete. I was screaming and crying while I tried to pull away from him.

"You stay away from him, bitch!" I screamed at Raven. "I'll kill you if you come near him again! You understand that??"

Raven was crying and shaking as she cowered behind Shard for protection. I wanted to get my hands on her so that I could do her some type of bodily harm. I realized even through my crimson rage that my blade had not made contact with her at all. Then I saw Shard holding his hand over his left arm. His face was set in a deep frown as he bit down on his bottom lip. I gasped when I saw the bright red blood streaming between his fingers.

"Ay, Shard," called Mal as he rushed over to him. "You ah-ight, man?"

"Yeah," Shard replied in a strained voice as he moved his left hand and inspected the wound. It was impossible to tell how deep it was because of all the blood that had seeped out. I put my hands up to my mouth. I suddenly felt nauseous.

Hutch had heard the ruckus from the beginning and had run back over to us without his female companion.

"You think you need to go to the hospital?" I heard him ask Shard.

"Nah," Shard managed to utter. "I don't think it's too bad. It's just ..." He stopped in midsentence as Mal took the do-rag from his head and tied it tight over the cut. "*Shit*," Shard hissed as the pain of the pressure coursed through his arm.

"What you think you're doing out here, Kyla?" Mal snapped as he turned on me. "You trying to kill somebody or something? See what you did? Now what if you had hurt yourself, too? Don't you realize you're pregnant, dammit? Or do you even care?" I was startled by the force of his anger.

Other people who had come out of the club had gathered around to stare.

"Ain't nothing to see!" yelled Mal, putting both hands in the air. "Ain't nothing to see here with this shit." As the crowd dispersed, Mal began to call out instructions.

"Hutch, get Kyla's keys and take her to the crib. I'm gonna stop Shard by the emergency room. That cut looks deep, and it's still bleeding."

"Nah, man," said Shard, shaking his head. "I'm ah-ight. It's not that bad." Even as he said those words, though, the look of agony on his face discredited his claims.

"We're going anyway," said Mal, disregarding Shard's wishes for once.

Hutch looked at me as everyone headed off to their respective destinations. "You ready?" he asked softly. I followed him slowly to the car, climbed into the passenger seat, and then leaned forward and placed my face in my hands.

"I wasn't trying to hurt *him*," I sobbed. "It was an accident."

Hutch was silent as he backed out of the parking space. I cried all the way home. I had gone back to the club to seek revenge on Raven and to make myself feel better. Instead, I had hurt Shard and made myself feel worse. When we got to the house, Hutch seated himself on the couch to wait for Shard and Mal to arrive. I went upstairs, ran a hot bath, and sank into the tub. I wondered how Shard was. The fact that I had injured the one person that I loved most terrified me. I mean, what was becoming of me?

After the bath, I got dressed in a nightshirt and climbed into bed. I slipped between the cool Egyptian cotton sheets and buried my face in the pillow. The pillowcase was soon soaked with my tears.

I had drifted into a restless snooze when I heard the bedroom door open and then close again. My eyelids fluttered open, and I sat up on the mattress. The lamplight on my nightstand was still burning softly. I watched apprehensively as Shard crossed the room and sat down on the edge of the bed. I glanced down at his forearm and saw that it was wrapped tightly and neatly with sterile white gauze that extended from right below his wrist to a couple of inches below his elbow.

"Baby," I whispered tearfully, "I wasn't trying to do that to you, I swear." He didn't reply. Instead, he stripped out of his shirt. I noticed the pained look on his face as he raised the injured arm over his head to slip the garment off.

"I'll get it for you," I said. I scampered off the mattress

as fast as my belly would allow. Then I rushed around to his side of the bed and dropped down to my knees and unlaced the strings on his Bally's. As I began to pull them off for him, he suddenly grabbed my wrist. I looked up into his eyes. They were filled with remorse and compassion.

"I'm sorry," he declared softly.

To say that I was shocked would be an understatement.

"Why? *I'm* the one who should be apologizing. I don't know why I—"

He shook his head. "Nah, that wasn't your fault. I hit you with some foul shit, and I expected you to just deal with it on your own. I was wrong." He tugged at my wrist until I rose slightly, and then I placed an apologetic kiss on his soft mouth. He returned it. "I'm sorry, okay?"

I sighed with relief. "Okay. And I'm sorry too."

Three

For the next week, I was frightened by the sight of my own reflection in the mirror. I didn't know who I was anymore. What had possessed me to grab that knife, drive across town, and attempt to stab my boyfriend's lover? Had it been the same force that had possessed me to swallow those sleeping pills in Mexico?

I no longer cared about the important things that had begun to matter to me—like my pregnancy. I was too worried about the status of my relationship with Shard to concern myself with thoughts of my own child. In order to assure that I wasn't losing him, I started following him around again, just to feel like I was still a part of his world. I knew that it definitely put a cramp in his style to have his pregnant girl riding on the passenger side whenever he went to handle his business. Still, I was right there with him, ready to ride or die for the cause.

I could tell that the crew was growing sick of me because they had to modify their behavior whenever I came around. They couldn't smoke in my presence. They had to censor what they said in front of me because everything made me angry or upset. My hormones were a mess; and the further along I got in my pregnancy, the worse I became.

Shard and Mal were the only two who ever dared to disagree with me about anything. Ever since the fiasco with the knife, I had heard guys in the crew calling me "crazy" and "deranged."

"Nah, man, she straight-up pulled a blade on the chick and tried to take her head off," I once heard Hutch whispering to an acquaintance at Mal's house party. "Shard puts it down on these girls. They always wig out over that nigga. I told him he needs to give me some of that game."

The friend had laughed loudly. "He would have to give you his face first, stupid. You couldn't never get it like Shard. You're too ugly!"

"Ah, man, go to hell," said Hutch with a good-natured laugh.

The two guys had suddenly grown quiet as I boosted myself off the wall that I had been leaning against and walked past them.

"What's going on, baby girl?" said Hutch with a grin as if he hadn't just talked trash about me less a minute earlier.

"You tell me," I sneered, rolling my eyes at him. I had

become very unlikable at that point. Even I couldn't deny that. I was unlikable because, in essence, I was so unhappy. I constantly picked myself apart, wondering why Shard felt such a need to go outside of our relationship for fulfillment.

I ran that question through my head over and over. I could never answer it. In actuality, the answer didn't matter so much to me, though. I only wanted him to keep loving me. I didn't want to lose everything that I had worked so hard to build with him. I wanted him to know that no matter what happened, I could still handle whatever went down in his life. If he could dish it, I could take it.

One week after the incident at Icy, Eli's new business partner called Shard to let him know that he was ready to deal. According to Shard, they had worked out all of the details of their exchange a couple of days earlier. Shard and I were sleeping soundly when he got the call a little after midnight on a Thursday. His ringing cell phone startled me awake.

I sat straight up in bed and groaned while he reached over to the nightstand and groggily answered. "What's up?" He listened silently for a moment. "Oh, word ..." He was quickly coming out of his semiconscious state. "We can handle that whenever, man ... You ready? Ah-ight, then ... How well you know your way around the city?"

Shard eased out of bed as he talked and grabbed his jeans from the wingback chair against the wall. He held the phone between his ear and shoulder blade as he pulled them on. "You know where Levine Road is?" he asked the caller. "Yeah. It's a motel on East Levine, at the very end. It's called Auburn

Palace. Just come out there in thirty, and we'll square it all away. Eli already told me what you were looking for. I'll let you see what I got ..."

As Shard talked, I climbed out of bed, too. "Where you going?" I mouthed, walking up to him.

He ignored me as he continued the conversation. "Ah-ight then," he said to his caller. "Just call me when you get there. It shouldn't take you more than about forty-five minutes from where you are now. Ah-ight." He hung up the phone and walked past me as he slipped on his T-shirt and then grabbed his jacket.

"Wait a minute." I rushed to follow him. "Where you going?"

"I gotta handle that deal that I told you about. I'll be back in a few hours." He stopped at the linen closet and pulled out his large black duffel.

"I'm going with you."

"No, you're not. You won't do nothing but get in my way. This is no place for you anyway."

"Why not?" I grabbed a pair of sweat pants out of my dresser drawer and stepped into a pair of sandals that I had left on the second-floor landing. "You let me go with you all the time before I got pregnant. Why you treat me like I'm a pest now? I won't slow you up."

"Stay here, Kyla."

"No. I'm coming with you. You said that you're going to a motel anyway. I'll just lie down and go to sleep while you do what you need to do. Just let me go with you."

He sighed as I followed him out into the garage.

"Whatever." He unlocked the Rover. Satisfied, I pulled the passenger-side door open and climbed inside.

Twenty-five minutes later, we arrived at the old courtyard motel that Shard had designated for the meeting with Eli's partner, a guy by the name of Sampson. When Shard unlocked the small room that he had rented, I stepped in behind him and looked around. It was like any other seedy motel room that I had seen. The carpet was old and thin. The curtains were faded. The walls were some strange shade of puke-green that made my already-weak stomach turn. I wandered over to the bed and perched on the edge, trying to make myself as comfortable as possible in the small, cramped space. I didn't even want to see what the bathroom looked like, but Shard was already approaching it. We had parked right behind the room, so the car would be visible from the bathroom. Shard took the big black duffel bag that he carried off his shoulder and placed it on the floor. Then he got down on his knees and ran a palm over the thin carpet.

"What are you doing?" I inquired as I watched him take a large pocketknife out of his back pocket and begin to tear a large square of carpet into a flap. Underneath the carpet was a dark brown wooden floor.

"This is the reason why I picked this place." Shard opened the bag and removed a large hammer and something that resembled a long, flattened ice pick. "They have wood floors."

He pushed the blunt end of the foreign-looking instrument into the edge of one of the strips of wood. Then he used the head of the hammer to pound the tool until the wood gave way and buckled under the pressure. After that, with his bare hands, he pulled the strip away from the floor. For several minutes he worked like this. By the time he was done, four strips had been torn away from the floor. There was a hollow space underneath, but the strips could be placed back on top to seal it off again. The pieces interlocked together so perfectly that to the untrained eye, it would appear that the floor had never even been damaged.

"What's all that for?" I asked.

"Just in case. You never can be too careful with these niggas that you don't know."

I realized then that Shard was a bit skeptical about Eli's guy as well. I had never seen him go to such lengths just to prepare for any potential trouble. I leaned back on one of my palms and placed my other hand over my belly while I watched him stand to his feet and remove his phone from his belt. He dialed a number, and then stepped outside of the door to talk. While he was outside, I got down on the floor and opened the bag to see what else it contained. Nestled inside were several thick white bricks of cocaine. On top of the bricks were several plastic baggies with hard rocks of crack inside. I zipped the bag and took my place on the bed again. Something about this whole scene didn't feel right to me. The situation was just too iffy. Shard was outside for nearly twenty minutes.

When he walked back into the room, he had a frown on his face. "I don't know what's taking him so long. He should've been here by now."

I rose slowly from the bed. "Maybe we should leave. If he ain't here on time, then it's just his loss. Let's get out of here."

Shard shook his head. "Not yet. Let me call Eli first and

see if he's heard anything from him."

Just as he opened his cell again, it started to chime. He flipped it open and retrieved the message. I watched apprehensively as he read the words that scrolled across the screen. The frown on his face disturbed me.

"What's wrong?" I anxiously asked. Standing up, I walked over to him and gazed down at the phone. Two words scrolled across the light blue screen: "BAD BUSINESS."

The message had come from Eli. It was cryptic, but Shard seemed to understand it.

"Come on." He grabbed the bag. "Let's ride."

I didn't have to be told twice. I led the way to the door. But as I grabbed the knob, I suddenly saw flashing blue lights sweep across the window from the outside. I looked back at Shard with wide eyes.

"Shit," he hissed. "We can't walk out of here with this." He dropped the bag, then stooped and proceeded to pull up the floorboards that he had jimmied loose. He worked at dropping the illegal products into the hollow space. I got down on my knees and began to pack the bricks tightly inside until they fit together like Legos. When we had the space filled, I ran to the window to look out. That was when I saw the two unmarked cars pulling into the motel parking lot. My knees wobbled, and I felt faint. Shard grabbed my arm and pulled me off to the bathroom.

I followed him and watched as he stood on the edge of the tub and hoisted the window on the wall behind it. "You gotta go through here, baby girl. This is the only other way out."

The window was small, but it was large enough for each

of us to slip through. I had to sit on the sill, duck my head underneath, and then pull myself out through the other side. I was extra careful, making sure that I didn't bump my stomach on the frame. As soon as I was outside, he tossed me the keys.

I hurried to pop the locks and jump into the driver's seat while he hopped through the window with minimal effort and dashed to the Rover. As soon as he was in the passenger seat, I peeled out of the lot and sped through the back exit, out of sight of the police around front.

"Slow down." Shard reached over to place a calming hand on my knee. "If you drive too fast, you're gonna attract attention. Just drive the speed limit."

I nodded and eased off the gas pedal until the car settled at fifty-five miles. Shard's phone started to ring, but he did not answer it.

"Where did those police come from?" I asked frantically. "How did they know what was going on? How did they know where we were?"

"Eli's boy is probably an informant." He sneered with disgust. "That figures." He looked up and suddenly seemed to realize that I was driving back toward Chesterfield. "Where you going? Hit the exit. We can't go back to the crib."

"Why not?"

"Kyla, they know what's going on. They been watching me all this time ... Probably police are crawling all around the house by now."

"What? What does that mean? What ... what's gonna happen now?" I started to struggle for breath.

"Nothing's gonna happen to you. You're good, so just relax."

"I'm not worried about me. I'm worried about you. Are they gonna arrest you? Why are they at our house?"

"They're probably searching it. I was preparing for this. My pops always told me to prepare at all times. That's why I been working so hard to stack up the extra cash."

"So what are we gonna do? Where are we going, to the east side?"

"Hell, no. I'm going to have to check into a hotel outside of the city for a minute. But you ... you're going to your folks."

"No! I'm not leaving you. And I'm *not* going back to those people!"

"Yes, you are."

"Shard, I wanna stay with you. I don't care what happens. If it happens to you, then it happens to me, too. I'm not leaving you."

He glanced in the rearview mirror to make sure that we weren't being followed. Shard remained calm as usual, seemingly unaffected by the fact that he was being pursued by the law. I didn't know what I would do if the police had dug up enough evidence to charge him. If he was locked up, I told myself that I would surely curl up and die. I drove us to University City, where Shard told me to stop at a payphone. Then, per his request, I hopped out, called Mal, and instructed him to meet us immediately at the Red Roof Inn there.

"Do you have any money on you?" I asked Shard as I climbed back into the Rover.

"Not a whole lot. That's why Mal's gotta come down there. He's been keeping track of all the accounts that we opened up in your name."

"*What*?" I looked at him. "What accounts?"

"This girl from the old neighborhood works down at Gateway Fidelity Bank, and she hooked us up. She just put everything in your name and changed up the mailing address a little bit so the money couldn't be traced back to the source. Big banks usually use outside companies to mail out statements, but the smaller banks mail the statements from in-house. We stashed the money in three small banks on different ends of the city where we knew people and greased their palms a little bit so that we could break up the deposits and not arouse suspicion. Our people would just hold the statements for us, and Mal would go and pick them up."

I was stunned. "How come you never told me that before?"

"Because if you had known how much money was sitting in the bank with your name on it, you might have gotten tempted to take it out and go on a spree or something."

"So you're saying that you trust Mal more than you trust me? You know that I would never take anything from you. I can't believe that you've been holding back on me for so long."

"It doesn't make any difference now," said Shard, "because I'm gonna have to take it out anyway and do something different. They'll be keeping a check on all of your financial activities now, too. We need to get a second signer on all those accounts—somebody whose hands are completely clean. Can you do that for me?"

"Yeah. No problem."

"We can talk about that later, though," he added as he looked down at his cell to receive the next incoming message. When we arrived at the parking lot of the Red Roof Inn, Mal was already there, faithful to the finish. He climbed out of his black Chevy Tahoe and met us halfway across the lot.

"I already checked in," he told Shard as he tossed him the key to the room. He had a concerned expression on his face. "I ain't gonna swear by this shit, nigga," said Mal as we all strolled quickly up the steps and to the room, "but I'm willing to bet my last two dollars that this dude that Eli sent down here is snitching for the Feds. He probably worked out a deal with them ma-fuckas, and then tipped you and Eli off at the last minute so nobody would try to retaliate. Eli hit me up right after he messaged you to tell me that he thinks the nigga's trying to take him down.

"The best thing that we can do right now is kite out until shit cools off. You know my cousin, Rob, is still in Miami. He said that his spot is always open to us. I think that would be our best bet right now." Shard nodded in agreement as he stuck the key in the lock and pushed the room door open.

"We need to get on that now," he told Mal. "Get rid of the Rover and get another ride ASAP." He popped the lights on in the room, and we all stepped inside. "I need to hit the highway before first light," he added. "They ain't got enough on you to run you in at this point. You can shut down shop out here, and then in a week, you can come on down there, too."

Mal nodded. "Sounds like a plan to me."

I sat down on a chair at the small desk in the room, rubbing my belly as I silently listened to them discuss their next moves. Were we actually going to Florida? I couldn't believe it! I immediately started to think of all the things that I had to do before we left town. Mal headed outside to use the payphone in the parking lot. He had begun to suspect that his phone may have been tapped as well.

"Shard," I said as I watched him fish his wallet out of his pocket and sift through the contents, "I'm already registered at Washington for next semester. They won't let me register for classes at another school until I take care of that. Maybe I could handle all that first thing in the morning, and then I could come to Miami tomorrow evening."

Shard shook his head as he slid his wallet back into his pocket. "You don't have to drop out of school, Kyla. That won't be necessary."

"I know that. I'm just dropping out of school *here*. I'll enroll at another college when I get to Florida."

Again, he shook his head. "You're not going to Florida. You're staying here."

"No," I said calmly. "I'm going. I'm not staying behind any longer than I have to. Why do I have to wait?"

He sighed. "You don't have to wait. You're not going— *period*."

I was floored by his declaration. "What?" I gripped the edge of the desk and hoisted myself to my feet. "What are you talking about? Wh—what do you mean?"

Shard suddenly lost his patience with me. "I mean that I can't take you, Kyla! Don't you understand that I'm risking everything just to get *myself* out of town? I'm not going on a damn vacation! This is my *life* we're talking about here!"

"So you're just gonna *leave* me?" I screamed as my face flushed and my eyes filled with tears. "You can't do that to me! Where am I supposed to go? What am I supposed to do?"

"You have a whole family here. You're gonna have to go home."

"I already told you," I sobbed, shaking my head. "I can't go back there. I don't even have a relationship with them anymore. I ain't got nobody but you."

"You're just gonna have to rectify the situation with your folks. You gotta go back and find a way to deal with it. At least until I can come back and get you."

"So when are you coming back? In a few weeks?"

He shook his head. "I don't think so. It's gonna be a little bit longer than that."

I walked up to him. "How much longer?"

He shrugged his shoulders. "A few months. Hopefully, no more than six or seven."

"*Six or seven months*? You can't leave me for that long, Shard! What am I supposed to do without you?" I clutched his shirttail. "You can't leave me! I swear I won't get in your way. I'll do whatever you need me to do. Whatever you want ... Just please don't leave me. Please!" The anguish in my voice came from the very depths of my soul. I honestly didn't believe that I could live without him. He was my lifeline. I was hysterical, and my breathing had started to come in spurts. The baby somer-saulted inside of me.

After a few seconds, Shard wrapped his arms around me. "Okay," he murmured soothingly in my ear. "Just calm down, ah-ight?" He rubbed my back and held me tightly. "I won't leave you here, okay?" We were still embracing him when Mal came back into the room.

"What's wrong?" he demanded as soon as he walked in and saw us.

"Nothing, man," said Shard. "It's cool." Mal nodded, and he and Shard exchanged looks.

Then Mal cleared his throat loudly. "Well," he said, "maybe y'all two oughta get a little bit of sleep before it's time to head out. I don't think that the trail is real hot right now, but before day breaks, we can be out of here." Shard nodded and gave Mal their signature solidarity hug and handshake. "I'll take your Rover so that they won't track you here," said Mal. "I'll be back in a few hours, ah-ight?"

"Ah-ight, man," said Shard. "I appreciate it."

"You know it's no problem," said Mal. He said good-bye to me, and then disappeared out the door. It had been an exhaust-ing couple of hours, and I was just looking forward to crawling into bed and getting a little sleep. Shard didn't even take off his clothes. He just kicked off his shoes and stretched out across the mattress. I popped off the light and then climbed onto the bed next to him, snuggling up close. For a while, I just lay in the dark, watching the wall as the reflection of passing vehicles fil-tered in through the vertical blinds at the large windows. I was tired, but I couldn't fall asleep. I had too much on my mind. I couldn't believe that I was about to leave St. Louis, the only home that I had ever known.

"Shard?" I called softly. "Are you asleep yet?"

"Uh-uh. I'm up."

"Are you scared?"

"Nah. Are you?"

"The only thing that scares me," I said, "is the thought of ever losing you for any reason. I won't lose you, will I?"

He hesitated before responding. The silence was so thick it could have been sliced with a knife. "You won't lose me," he finally replied. He hadn't answered quickly enough to put my mind completely at ease, but I drifted into a deep but troubled sleep anyway.

All that night I was plagued by strange nightmares and senseless dreams. I didn't wake up, though. I just continued to sleep through the series of mental imageries. Just after the crack of dawn, the sunlight gently caressed my eyelids until they fluttered open. The atmosphere was so peaceful, I nearly forgot about all of the events of the previous night. Suddenly, reality came crashing down on me. I sat straight up with a gasp, remembering that Shard and I had been planning to leave the hotel before daybreak.

I could hear a steady stream of water splashing into the sink in the bathroom.

"Shard?" I called, rising with my big belly and standing to my feet. I stepped to the closed door and rapped on it with my knuckles. "We're supposed to be gone by now, aren't we?" I listened as the water stopped running. "I think Mal's late. You want me to go to the payphone outside and call him?"

I waited for a response, then heard him moving toward the door. The knob turned, and the door slowly swung open. I took two steps back, stunned by who I saw standing there.

It was Mal.

I frowned in confusion. "Hey, Mal. When did you get here?"

He looked down at his hands while he dried them on a small white towel. "I been here a couple of hours. I was waiting for you to wake up."

"Where's Shard?"

Mal clutched the towel tightly in his hands and waved toward the bed. "Sit down for a second," he said. I noticed that he was barely able to make eye contact with me.

"I don't wanna sit down. What's going on?"

"Man, I always gotta do the dirty work," he mumbled to himself, shaking his head.

"What dirty work? Stop stalling, Mal. Where's Shard?"

Since Shard and I had been together, Mal had witnessed quite a bit of drama from the two of us. He had always been the one who tried to bring peace and harmony between us. He had seen a lot of the pain that the relationship had caused me. It was for all those reasons that I had often seen a look of sympathy, compassion, and affinity in his eyes when he had gazed at me. This time, though, I saw something so different. This time, Mal looked at me with pity.

"I'm gonna ask you one more time," I said as my throat

began to tighten and my face started to burn, "where is he?"

Mal took a deep, preparatory breath and then swallowed hard. "Kyla, you know he couldn't take you with him." He shook his head again. "I'm sorry to have to tell you this, baby girl, but ... Shard is gone."

Four

I don't think that I reacted in quite the way that Mal had expected. As soon as he delivered the news about Shard's departure, I
saw him brace himself. His whole body tensed, and he stared at
the far wall, waiting for my emotional breakdown. I just stared
at him, though, still trying to understand what he had said to me.
Still trying to understand what was happening. There was no way
that Shard had just up and left me. He knew that I was all alone.
He knew that nobody in the world mattered to me like he did. If
he knew those things, there was no way that he would leave me.
I kept telling myself that there was just no way.

    "So ... he's gone to Florida already?" I asked Mal. "He
just got up and left while I was sleeping?"

    "He didn't have no other choice. He knew that there was

no way you would let him leave without causing a scene."

"But … he told me that he wasn't gonna leave me," I said robotically. I perched on the edge of the bed. "Well, when am I going to Florida? Am I supposed to go down there with you next week?"

Mal leaned back against the wall and stuck his hands in his pants pockets. "You still don't get it," he mumbled as he observed the hopeful expression on my face. He sat down next to me and rubbed his hand over his chin. "You aren't going. The only reason that he said you could go was because he didn't want you to flip out. We know how you react in certain situations, Kyla. He was just trying to get you to sleep through the night."

My eyes began to swim with tears. "No. I know he didn't just leave me like this. He *didn't*."

"He had to," said Mal. "The Feds are onto him. Pretty soon, they're gonna be onto me and the rest of the crew, too. What you want Shard to do? Stick around here and wait to get hauled off to prison with his daddy and brothers? At least if he leaves town, he's got a fighting chance at not getting caught up. He's a wanted man now. That isn't going to be easy for him. It's not gonna be easy for any of us. That's the life that we all chose, though. We knew what came along with the territory when we went for broke and got into this game. I know that you'll miss him, and it's gonna be hard to accept all this at once. But believe me, cooperating is the best thing that you can do for him right now." I nodded my head at Mal's words. Then I placed my face in my hands.

I knew I had to be understanding. I had to be the type of

woman that I had been for Shard for the past two years. The type of woman who always put her own needs aside in order to support her man in whatever he needed to do. I couldn't cry in front of Mal. I wanted him to tell Shard that I had been a pillar of strength.

"This will all eventually blow over, baby girl," said Mal. "Before you know it, y'all will be right back together."

So just like that, I was left with nothing. No man. No home. No car. No money. No visible means of support. I had nothing but the clothes on my back. I couldn't even go back to the house to grab any extra clothing because Mal said that the property was still being monitored—probably even more closely than it had been before.

"You don't even have to answer any questions if anybody else comes up to you," he told me later that day as he drove me back to my old neighborhood. "Shard made sure that you didn't get caught up in any mess. No matter what anybody tells you, you're clean. They don't have any dirt on you, so don't let them intimidate you or bully you into giving up any info, ah-ight?"

"Okay."

I gazed out of the window at all of the familiar scenery that whizzed by. It had been so long since I had been back in this area. Nothing had changed.

I sat there on the passenger side of Mal's ride while he chauffeured me, wondering what I was going to say to my estranged family. I wracked my brain, trying to decide on my first words. I wondered how they would react to me. Knowing them, I guessed that they would scorn me. Call me stupid for letting love take me over the way that it had. I was certain that they wouldn't believe me if I tried to tell them that Shard and I were still going to be together, that all this mess was merely a temporary hurdle.

"When will I talk to him?" I asked Mal as he turned the truck onto Granny's block. "How can I call him? Will he call me to give me a number?"

"Not right now. For the next month or so, they're gonna be watching all of us like hawks. We have to be extra careful with how we handle things. Whenever I hear from Shard, I'll let you know, though, okay?"

"As soon as you hear from him?"

"Yeah," he promised. He pulled to a halt by the curb at Granny's house.

I gazed out at the small green lawn. I noticed that the curtains at the living-room windows were different, and someone had replaced the faded old numbers on the facade of the house with shiny new ones.

"What if I really need Shard for some reason?" I asked Mal as I continued to stare out of the window, trying to fight back the fresh tears. "What if I just need to hear his voice? What do I do?"

"You have to tell me. If it's a bona fide emergency, I'll get in touch with him for you."

"Do me one favor," I asked.

"Just name it."

"Tell him that I love him. And that I understand."

"Consider it done. Just be sure that you don't go back to

the house or to the apartment in East. Don't worry about your dog. I'll get him out of there and have him taken care of, ah-ight?"

I nodded, but I remained planted in the seat, my fingers wrapped around the door handle. I was so afraid to walk up that stoop and knock on the door. I felt like just remaining there in the vehicle with Mal until Shard's return. At that point, Mal was my only link to Shard. I wanted to hold on tight to whatever was left. Mal was sympathetic to my plight. He didn't rush me to get out of the SUV.

He just sat patiently, waiting for me to make my move. "I know how much heart you got, Kyla. You're gonna need that now more than ever. Keep your head up, okay?"

I just nodded. It was becoming harder to hold the tears back, so I pushed the door open and clumsily climbed out of the vehicle. I closed the door behind me and trudged slowly up the walkway that led to the house. It was a lonely, scary journey. When my foot touched the bottom step of the stoop, I looked back one last time at Mal. He had shifted into drive and was already pulling away. I turned again and climbed the remaining steps. It had seemed like an eternity since I had last climbed those steps. I ran my hand over the wooden railing on the small front porch, allowing my fingertips to slide over the "Kyla B Wuz Here" that I had carved there when I was ten years old. A soft sigh escaped my lips.

Kyla B is back again, I thought.

Bravely, I stepped up to the door and rapped on the glass pane in the wood, biting down on my bottom lip while I waited for a response. I nervously wrung my hands. The lock suddenly clicked, and then the doorknob turned. I looked up in time to see my little cousin, Will, standing there, chomping on a piece of bubble gum and holding a video game in his hands. I marveled briefly over the growth spurt he'd had since I had last seen him. I couldn't believe that he was already nine years old. Before I had left home, I had practically been given complete charge over him by his momma, Jazz.

His eyes grew wide behind the lenses of his glasses when he saw me. "Hey, Kyla."

"Hey. How you doing?"

"Fine." He looked down at my belly, then he pushed his glasses up the bridge of his nose and continued to gawk at me. "Where you been? Why did you leave?"

My patience was running low with him. I was already stressed out about everything that was going on in my life. I didn't feel like an interrogation. "What difference does it make, Will?"

He looked startled by my response. "I don't know. I just missed you. That's all."

I immediately felt bad for the way that I had responded to him. "I ... I missed you, too." I stared past him and into the living room. "Where's Granny?"

"At her beauty shop. My momma's in the back, though." My heart plummeted to my feet. How was I supposed to face Jazz? What would I say to her? Will held the door open wider. "Are you coming in?" he asked me.

I looked over my shoulder as if I expected Mal to pull

back up at that moment and take me back to Chesterfield. I turned again to face Will. "Yeah."

I swallowed hard as he stepped aside, allowing me to walk into the living room. Then I just stood there awkwardly, taking in every tiny detail. Granny had redecorated. There was a new sofa, love seat, and recliner. New carpeting. New figurines and what-nots on the shelves and coffee table. I couldn't help but wonder whether it had been her latest sugar daddy, or Jazz's, who had financed the face-lift. I didn't even feel comfortable here anymore. Everything was so foreign and strange to me. I didn't sit. I actually felt that it would be rude of me to sit without being invited.

"Will?" I heard Jazz call from down the hallway. "Baby, who was at the ..."

Her sentence trailed as she came around the corner and saw me standing there. Her steps came to a halt as well. She was dressed in old shorts and a T-shirt. She wore a white bandana tied over her head. She looked exactly the same. Still the beauty she had always been.

I saw her eyes immediately fall to my belly. "Kyla."

I sucked my teeth and gazed off in the distance. "How you doing?" Before she could respond, I added, "When will my granny be home?"

Jazz looked around as if Granny may have been standing right behind her. "I don't know. She's at the shop right now. You know you're welcome to wait for her, though."

Unexpectedly, my eyes glazed over with tears. "I don't have any other choice. I don't have anywhere else to go."

Jazz furrowed her brow. "What do you mean?"

The tears finally broke free and coursed down my face. "I mean that I don't have a place to live. He's gone, and he left me all by myself. I don't have money or clothes. I ain't got nothing."

"Oh, Kyla." Jazz crossed the room. I saw the concern in her eyes as she grabbed me by the shoulders and pulled me to her. I laid my forehead on her shoulder and wept until I was almost convulsing. Now that my tears had broken free, it was impossible to bottle them up again.

She held me tightly and ran her hands over my hair. "You still have us, girl. We're here for you. You *always* have us."

Returning home did a real number on my pride. The strange thing about it all, though, was that nobody in my family tried to demoralize me about my situation. Nobody tried to make me feel small for the way that things had played out between me and my relatives. In fact, they did the exact opposite. They coddled me. They pampered me. Especially Jazz. I couldn't even hold any more malice toward her after the way that she had comforted me. She even took it upon herself to buy me some maternity clothes and a few pairs of comfortable shoes.

Granny was thrilled to have me home. When she had walked through the door that first day and discovered me lying on the sofa, she had grabbed me and hugged me so tightly, I thought that she would cut off my air supply. All she could talk about was the baby. She rubbed my belly and talked soothingly to it, promising the little person inside of me that if I ever tried to keep him or her away again, she would strangle me.

Will had to sleep in the living room at night, because he had taken my old bedroom when I had left home. When I returned, he had been forced to relocate. I had assured him that the arrangement wouldn't be permanent, though. I was going to be back with Shard in only a matter of months. I told Granny that. I told Jazz that. I told everybody. This was only temporary. Nobody ever disputed my claims. They only listened, and then nodded in response.

I knew what they were thinking. They were thinking that I was being foolish to hold onto him after he had left me there penniless. I didn't expect them to understand, though. They would never be able to relate to the deeply spiritual bond that Shard and I shared. I knew that bond would always bring us back together. That bond would never allow him to forget about me or the promise that he had made to come back for me.

After three days, I still hadn't heard anything from Mal. I began to worry that Shard had not arrived at his destination safely. My nights were racked with constant worry. I tossed and turned all over my old full-sized bed until I was tangled up in the sheets. I often felt the baby moving around inside of me, rendered just as restless as I was.

I was afraid to contact Mal or anyone else in the crew. I did not want to do anything that would jeopardize Shard's well-being. I didn't know if the Feds had tapped other phones. I didn't know how many other people they had under surveillance. Whenever I ventured outside of the house to go to class or take quick trips to the store, I was constantly looking over my shoulder, constantly wondering if anybody was watching me.

One afternoon, I drove Jazz's car to the elementary school to pick up Will for her. I was sitting there, gazing out the windshield at the kids as they poured out onto the schoolyard and ventured beyond the fence to board the school bus or climb into their parents' respective vehicles. I watched some of the boys annoying the girls by yanking at their ponytails or snatching their backpacks from their shoulders.

"STOP, BOY!!!" a girl screamed angrily. *"YOU GET ON MY NERVES! SHOOT!"* I just shook my head and chuckled, remembering how boys had done those same things to me, back when they had been too young and immature to admit that they liked me. I was caught up in my recollections when a tap at the window startled me back to the present.

I turned and gazed out to see Hutch standing there. I thought I was hallucinating.

I was too anxious to roll the window down, so I just grabbed the handle and pushed the door open and climbed out, looking at him expectantly.

"What's up, baby girl?" He peered at me from underneath the bill of his St. Louis Cardinals cap. "How you doing?"

I ignored his greeting. "How is Shard? Is he okay? Did he make it to Miami all right?"

"Yeah, he's just fine. Mal sent me to your grandmother's house, but your aunt told me that you had come out here." He began to dig into the pocket of his jeans. "Mal told me to give you this." He produced a slip of folded white paper. "He left this morning for Florida, but he said he wanted to make sure that he made contact with you."

"Thanks." I accepted the paper from him.

"I'm heading out of here first thing tomorrow morning," Hutch informed me. "Me and Shorty are going to California."

"Y'all are? For good?" I asked.

Hutch nodded. "Shit is getting too critical here. It's time to move on." He placed a hand on my shoulder. "You take care of yourself, ah-ight?"

"You, too."

I climbed back into the car and began to open the paper with shaky hands. Once it was unfolded, I turned it right-side up. I had to squint to make sense of Mal's small handwriting, but I managed to decipher it:

> Kyla,
>
> I'll be at the spot by the time you get this. Things are good as gold. Be by the phone at EXACTLY 7:00 tonight. It's important.

My heart started pounding like a steel drum. I glanced at the clock on the instrument panel. It was 3:17.

I nearly jumped out of my skin when Will pulled the passenger-side door open and climbed into the car. "Hey, Kyla."

"Hey."

"My friends over there talking 'bout you," said Will. "They said you're pretty." He pointed out the windshield to a group of three nine-year-old boys hanging near the bus stop. They were all staring into the car, practically drooling. When I looked at them, they quickly turned their heads and pretended that they had been looking in the other direction.

I shifted into drive and pulled away from the curb. "Did

you tell them that I look like Humpty-Dumpty when I stand up?" I asked as I looked down at my belly.

Will nodded his head. "Yep, I told 'em."

I shook my head and chuckled. As I drove, my mind automatically went back to Mal's note, which I was clutching tightly in my sweaty palm. I wondered what he needed to talk to me about. Maybe something really *had* happened to Shard, but Mal hadn't had the heart to tell me on paper. By the time I pulled up at Granny's house fifteen minutes later, I was a nervous wreck.

Jazz walked into the living room. "Kyla, a guy came by here looking for you."

"He found me," I told her. She looked curious, but she didn't ask any questions.

For the rest of the afternoon, I was on pins and needles. I jumped up and dashed to the phone every time it rang. All kinds of horrible scenarios raced through my mind. Images of Shard in handcuffs as the police whisked him off to the nearest prison. Images of him barely surviving in some rat-infested, below-poverty-level ghetto as he hid out from the authorities. Or worse. What did Mal have to talk to me about? The digital clock in my bedroom read 6:59 when I finally got my call. The cordless phone receiver had been resting on my lap, and I grabbed it and pressed the power button midway through the first ring.

"Hello?" I frantically answered as I tightly gripped the receiver, waiting to hear Mal's greeting on the other end of the line.

"What's up?"

"*Shard?*" My breath started to come out in short, spo-radic pants.

"Yeah. It's me, baby girl. How you doing?"

"No. How are *you* doing? Are you okay? Are you safe?"

"I'm all right."

"You sound so good," I said as tears dripped from my chin. "I been waiting over a week for somebody to tell me something. I just wanted to know that you were okay."

"I'm calling from a prepaid cell, and I'm gonna toss it after this, so I can't talk long." He paused. "Are you crying?"

"I can't help it. I just miss you so much. I want to be with you."

"You will. When the time is right, I promise you that we'll be together. With everything being so hot right now, I had to get my shit together. That was what you wanted anyway, wasn't it?" I realized that Shard was coding his words in case other ears were listening. He was telling me that he had gone legit.

I sat up straighter on the bed. "So everything's cool? You're not ... in the business anymore?"

"Nah. I gotta cut it loose for now. Maybe you were right. Maybe it is time to get my priorities in order. As soon as I get myself straight here, I'll send for you. You just gotta let me iron some things out first, okay?"

"Okay." I sighed with relief. I was suddenly filled with more hope than I had ever had before. Shard and I could have a normal life together! If he was getting out of the game, then I knew that things would be perfect when we were finally reunit-ed. I didn't have time to rejoice, though, because as usual, he was ready to get straight down to business.

"You remember what we talked about before I left?" he asked. "About the business that I needed you to take care of?" I realized that he did not want to go into detail over the phone. I knew that he was speaking about the money, though. The bank accounts.

"Yeah, I remember."

"Well, it's time to do that. I'll get you everything that you'll need to take care of it. You're a real intelligent girl; so I know you can hold it down for me."

"I'll handle everything."

"Good." We were both silent for a moment. "Well, I should go," he finally said. "But I'll get you what you need real soon, ah-ight?"

"Okay." My tears started to flow again. I didn't want to hang up the phone. I wanted his voice to float through the receiver until it lulled me to sleep. I didn't want to let him go again. "You know I love you, right?" I asked.

"Yeah. I love you, too." He sighed. "I'll talk to you later."

"When?" I asked, but he had already hung up.

I lay down on my side and sobbed until my throat and my stomach hurt. The baby started moving violently. I looked down at my belly and saw the imprint of a tiny fist poking through my skin. I stared at it in fascination until it moved away. I placed my hand on my stomach and rubbed it until all was quiet again.

"Are you trying to tell me something?" I asked softly. It was the first time I had ever actually spoken to the bulge in my belly. "Am I upsetting you?" I continued to rub the skin tenderly. I had read in a parenting magazine that an unborn baby experienced everything that the mother experienced. I had thought that this only pertained to the physical, but I began to wonder if it was emotional, too. "If you are feeling my pain, I am so sorry," I told the baby. "I wouldn't wish this kind of misery on *anybody*."

Two days later, I received a small package in the mail. There was no return address written on it. I took the package and carried it to the safety of my bedroom, where I closed and locked the door. Using my nails, I quickly tore through the tape and cardboard. When I reached inside, I discovered a large Ziploc bag. I opened the bag and turned it upside-down so that all of the contents spilled onto the bed, then I carefully sorted through all of the items. Among them were two bank cards, bank books, personal checkbooks, financial statements, and other information pertaining to the accounts that Shard had opened. Just as he had told me, my name was on everything. As I examined one of the statements, I heard a knock at the door.

"Kyla?" called Granny.

I quickly grabbed the materials and stuffed them back into the bag. "Just a minute!" I slipped the bag underneath the bed and then stood and opened the door.

"Hey," said Granny. "Come on in the kitchen. Dinner's ready."

"I'm not hungry. Thanks anyway."

"What do you mean, you're not hungry? Now you know that you need to eat something. You haven't been looking too good these last couple of days. You look peaky and tired."

"I'm fine. I've just been having a little trouble resting at night."

She reached out to lay a hand on my belly. "This little one been moving around a lot? Keeping you up?"

"Sometimes."

Granny propped her other hand up on the door frame. "Maybe you ought to take a little break from school, Kyla. It can't be good for you to be walking across that big campus every day with all those books, squeezing into those small desks ... Plus, you're always studying, writing papers, or reading something. You're almost seven months pregnant now. Why don't you just let school go until you've had the baby and gotten some rest?"

I shook my head and tried to give her a smile. "It's okay, Granny. I'll just go to bed a little bit earlier every night. Anyway, I can't leave school right now. The semester's only half over. I need to get as many credit hours as I can because when I go to where Shard is, I'll have to register at another school. I don't want to spend three extra years trying to graduate. The sooner I finish these classes, the sooner I can get my degree."

Granny nodded slowly, but her eyebrow was raised and her head was cocked to the side. "I'm just concerned about you," she said. "Health problems can sneak up on you before you even realize that anything is wrong. Believe me. You don't look well. Jazz has noticed it. Denise and Monica have noticed it, too."

"I'm fine, Granny. I'll be in the kitchen in five minutes to get something to eat, okay?"

"All right."

She gave me one last look before she turned and headed back down the hallway. I closed the door again and walked back over to the bed to retrieve the information. I didn't understand why my grandmother was stressing so hard. I had been a little fatigued lately, but I didn't feel that it was anything to be alarmed about.

The next day I called Nina to the house to tell her that I needed a favor from her.

"What's up, girl?" she asked.

"Would you go with me to the bank? I want you to add you to some bank accounts." I had known that Nina would be confused when I came to her with the request.

"You want me on your accounts? Why?"

I was reluctant to give her too much information. I knew that if she knew too much, she would refuse to help me. Though nobody talked about it, the whole family had a pretty good idea of why Shard had left. Everybody in St. Louis and East St. Louis knew about it. Word had gotten around.

"The thing is, they're investigating Shard. I have money, but I don't want the Feds to think it's linked to him. They could seize all of his assets. If I have you on the accounts with me, they'll believe that the money is mine and yours. They wouldn't touch it if it was linked to you. You don't have anything at all to do with Shard."

"Why would they take *your* money?" she asked. "You didn't do anything wrong, did you?"

"No." I sat down next to her on the edge of my bed as I

lowered my voice another notch so that nobody else in the house could hear me. "But they know that me and Shard are together. We lived in the same house. They may try to use that to keep me from getting to my money. I just need you as a safeguard."

Nina was reluctant to comply. "Could I get in trouble?"

"Girl, no. I wouldn't put you in a shady situation, girl. You know better."

"Okay," she finally agreed. "I'll do it."

The next day, Nina and I went down to the three different banks, and I added her to all of the accounts. Once we were seated in her car, she looked at me with wide eyes. "How much money was in all those?" she asked.

"All together, about $200,000."

It was Shard's backup money. The money he had been setting aside in case of an emergency. I began to wonder if I could really trust Nina to keep her hands off the funds. Looking at the dreamy glaze over her eyes made me worry.

"Nina, you cannot dip into that money for any reason whatsoever. That means you can't decide to grab a couple hundred to go and buy some shoes or something. It's off-limits. The only time you can ever touch it is when I tell you that I need you to withdraw some for me."

"I'm not a thief. I wouldn't ever steal from you. Damn, girl. Cut me some slack."

"This is between me and you then, right?" I questioned. "You can't tell your momma, Granny, or anybody else."

"I know. I won't say anything. I swear."

Nina was my last resort. I didn't have any other choice.

I had to trust her.

For the next few weeks, I got several phone calls from Shard or from Mal calling on Shard's behalf. They would instruct me to have a certain amount of money transferred to a mysterious account in Jacksonville, Florida. I would then call Nina and repeat the instructions. She would, in turn, carry them out. She was always suspicious as to why I was wiring money to Florida. She didn't ask too many questions, though. She was reliable, too. Sometimes Shard would ask for an amount as small as a thousand dollars. At other times, he would ask for slightly more. Whatever the amount, though, I could count on Nina to send it down to the exact penny as soon as I made the request.

For about five weeks, things went smoothly, without a single hitch.

One cold February afternoon as I rode the bus home from class, I started to feel strange. My lower abdomen ached. Almost like the cramps I had experienced during my menstrual cycle when I had been younger. It was nothing overwhelming, though, so I disregarded it. When I arrived home, the house was empty. Granny and Jazz were both working, and Will was still at school. I dropped my books on the couch and headed into the kitchen to wash the breakfast dishes that had accumulated that morning. I had just dropped the last plate into the hot, soapy water when I heard a knock at the front door. Drying my hands, I trudged through the living room and pulled the door open. Standing there on the porch was Denise. And she didn't look happy.

"Hey," I started to greet her. She put her hand up to

silence me before I could go on. Then, she brushed past me and stormed into the house. I closed the door behind her and then turned to see her standing in the center of the room with her hands on her hips.

"Kyla," she said in a husky voice, "I want you to know that I have never judged you or any of the choices that you've made in your life. Whenever anybody tried to question the things that you did, I would just shut my mouth and keep my two cents out of it. I know that you're a grown woman now, and so is Nina. But this time ... this time, I have to speak."

I frowned in confusion as I watched her reach into her shoulder bag and remove three small vinyl booklets, bound together by a tan rubber band. A closer look at them revealed that they were the checkbooks for the accounts.

"I found these in Nina's dresser drawer when I was putting away her laundry." Denise waved the booklets like a church fan. "For the life of me, I couldn't understand where she had gotten this type of money from. When she came home from work, I questioned her about it. She just kept coming up with one pitiful lie after another. When I didn't buy any of it, she finally broke down and told me that she was keeping it for you."

I opened my mouth to try to explain, but she held her hand up to silence me again.

"I know that this money is connected with that ... that man. Someway, somehow, I know that it's connected to him." She shook her head and looked at me in disbelief as she tossed the bundle onto the coffee table. "Nina is your cousin, Kyla. You grew up together. You've been closer than sisters. Why would you want to put her in this position? Why would you ask her to do something like this?"

"It's not like that," I finally managed to protest. "Shard is legit now. He's not out there doing the things that he was doing before. He started over with a clean slate, but he can't do it without some help. All I asked Nina to do was sign on the account. It's not that big of a deal."

"*Not that big of a deal*??" Denise was shouting now. "It's a *huge* deal, Kyla! See, what you fail to understand is that the decisions that you make in your life don't just affect you. They affect everybody in this whole family, because you drag everybody else into the issues that you have with him. I'm tired of walking on eggshells around you. I'm tired of tiptoeing around this subject. He ain't no good, Kyla. He never has been. Ever since the day that you brought him to this house, I knew that he wasn't no damn good. And the simple fact that he would even ask you to do some shit like this should prove that to you!"

"Shut up!" I screamed, startling her into silence. "You don't know him! You don't know shit about him, or what he's been through. He loves me. And as soon as he gets himself straight, we're gonna be together. He made some mistakes in the past, but he's ready to change the way he's living."

"And why is he so ready to change all of a sudden? Is it because he's on the verge of getting thrown in the penitentiary with the rest of his no-good-ass family?"

"Shut up, Denise!" I was so angry, I felt like I was about to erupt. All the heat rose to my face and my eyes blurred with tears of rage. "You need to—"

My words came to a screeching halt as a hot pain sliced through my abdomen. It was so excruciatingly deep, I wondered if I might have swallowed some caustic substance. I let out a scream of agony as I doubled over and sank to the floor, clutching my belly. It suddenly felt like I was urinating on myself.

Denise rushed over to me. "What's wrong? Kyla? *Kyla? What's wrong?*" I couldn't even respond to her. All I could do was curl up in the fetal position on the floor and cry. I vaguely heard my aunt begging me to try to stand up and walk out to her car. And then the pain must have gotten too intense for me.

That was when I passed out.

Five

When I opened my eyes again, I was lying flat on my back, staring up at a white sterile ceiling that was lined with fluorescent lights. My head pounded furiously, and when I tried to rise up, it felt like it weighed a hundred pounds. My lower body felt so strange. I couldn't feel anything below my waist. My mouth and throat were as dry as cotton.

"Kyla?" I suddenly heard a slightly strange, yet slightly familiar male voice utter. "Kyla, honey, how are you? You feeling okay?"

My eyes darted all around as I tried to find the body to which the voice belonged. Suddenly, Denise was staring down at me, her brow knit with deep concern.

"Answer the doctor, Kyla," she said, speaking to me as if

I was a small child. "Let him know if you're feeling better now."

I parted my lips to speak, but my throat was so parched, it felt as if it would crack. Instead of speaking, I just nodded my head.

"What ... happened?" I finally managed to murmur.

"You're at the hospital," said Denise. "You fainted, and I called an ambulance. I thought that you were threatening a miscarriage."

Her words petrified me. Immediately, my hand went down to my belly. "Did I have a ..."

I was afraid to even finish the sentence. Denise gave me a comforting smile. Then she reached down and stroked my hair. "No. The baby just decided to show up a little early. Dr. Lansky said that you went into premature labor. They're not exactly sure why, but they think your blood pressure may have had something to do with it."

"That's right, Kyla," said the voice again.

I felt my upper body being elevated until I was practically in a sitting position. I was suddenly able to get a full view of the room that I was in. I looked down and saw that I was dressed in a thin white hospital gown. My feet had been placed in metal stirrups so that my legs were wide apart. My obstetrician, Dr. Lansky, was sitting on a stool looking underneath the sheet that had been spread over my lower body. I realized that the voice I had been hearing belonged to him. There was a uniformed young white woman lingering near him. She gave me a warm smile. I guessed that she was Dr. Lansky's nurse.

"How did I get in this gown?" I asked, looking down at

my garb again.

"You put it on when we got here," answered Denise. "You came to once, but you went out again when Dr. Lansky gave you anesthesia for the pain."

"How can I be in labor?" I moaned as tears gathered in my eyes. "It's not time yet. It's only been seven months."

"Don't you worry about that, honey," said Dr. Lansky from behind the surgical mask that he wore. "We're going to do everything in our power to make sure that this baby has a fighting chance. All right?"

I didn't hear anything that he said, though. The realization that I was having a premature baby hit me like a fist in the stomach. How could a child born so early survive? Would it be normal and healthy, or would it need constant medical care for life? I began to panic, and soon, I was sobbing. That was when I realized how much I wanted my baby. That was the moment that I realized how much I had loved it all along.

"Kyla," Denise, placed an arm over my shoulder, "you gotta be strong now. You have to believe that this baby's gonna be okay." She planted a kiss on my sweaty forehead. "I called everybody already. Your granny is on her way over here from work. Camille said that she was taking the next flight in; and as soon as Jazz picks up Will from school, she's gonna take him to Nina, and then she's coming, too. Everybody's pulling for this child. It's gonna be okay. You *have* to believe that." Despite her courageous words, I saw the tears that filled her eyes. "It was because of me," she added. "I shouldn't have upset you like I did."

I shook my head and wiped my tears. "No, it was me. I was hurting earlier today, and I didn't say anything about it. I should have said something."

In reality, all I could think about was the Zolpidem that I had swallowed in my botched suicide attempt in Cancun. My heart told me that it was indeed *I* who had harmed my baby.

It was my fault. It was all my fault.

I had never felt so guilty in my life. The mere possibility that I might have caused harm to my unborn child or greatly lowered its quality of life was too much for me to handle.

By the time my granny arrived in the room, all scrubbed up and dressed in hospital garb, I was an emotional mess. Denise left me with Granny, saying that she had to go and take a breather. She looked absolutely distraught.

Granny's soothing touch was a million times better than any anesthesia; and her firm, yet soft words of encouragement were far more effective than the doctor's coaching. Though the beginning of the labor had been excruciating, the delivery was actually easy when contrasted with the horror stories that I had often heard. I guess it was because my lower body was numb. I didn't even have to push. The doctor delivered the baby through a method called "vacuum extraction."

I was so sedated I could barely keep my eyes open, but I heard the small, shrill screams ring out over the room. After that, I heard Granny laugh, and then I heard Dr. Lansky declare, "He's got a great set of lungs on him!"

"*Him*?" I turned my head to look at Granny. "It's a boy?"

She nodded as she marveled at the precious cargo I had

just delivered.

"*Ohhh*," she crooned. "Look how gorgeous he is, Kyla. Look at him."

I turned my head again to see the nurse clipping the umbilical cord as Dr. Lansky held the slimy little thing up for me to see. He was red, and his mouth was gaped wide open, showing off small pink gums as he continued to scream. He was so tiny. He looked so helpless and fragile.

"Lemme hold him," I slurred. "I wanna hold him." Dr. Lansky ignored me and started to whisk the baby out of the room. "Where are they going with my baby?" I asked Granny frantically as I tried to sit up. "Where they taking him?"

Granny held her arms around me. "Shh, Kyla. It's okay. Let them do what needs to be done for him. He'll be fine."

I started to yell out for them to bring my child back. I couldn't muster the energy, though. All I could do was lie back, close my eyes, and sleep.

My son entered my world on February 12th, two days before Valentine's Day. He had weighed only 4 pounds. He had to be placed in an incubator, and he was kept under intensive supervision for almost three full days. The doctors said that his heartbeat was remarkably strong, and all of his organs were functioning as well as those of a full-term baby.

He was a fighter. Everybody realized that from day one.

I was afraid to go down to the maternity ward and look at him. I was afraid that he would be so small that my heart wouldn't be able to take it. I lay there for two and a half days and stared up at the ceiling, ignoring the nurse while she begged me to eat the tray of food that she had brought to me.

Each of my relatives came into the room at one time or another to tell me how beautiful the baby was. I was afraid that they were all only trying to make me feel better, though. I believed that they were all secretly blaming me for not taking better care of myself while I was pregnant. Deep inside, I felt that I had caused the spontaneous premature delivery of my child.

It wasn't until Camille was sitting in the room with me, staring blankly at the TV, that the nurse finally brought him in to me. He had been washed clean and was wrapped in a white and blue-striped receiving blanket. He wore a little blue cotton cap on his head.

"Ooh, bring him over here," crooned Camille as she opened her arms to the nurse. Camille had already seen him earlier, but she was eager to hold him.

"No," I intercepted. "Bring him to me first. I didn't even get a good look at him yet."

The nurse smiled as she walked over, cradling him warmly to her bosom. "Young lady, you have a gorgeous baby," she purred. "All the nurses downstairs have fallen in love with him. Take good care of him. He's going to bring you so much joy." She began to lay him in my waiting hands. "Use this hand to cradle his body and this one to support his head."

Once I was holding him correctly, I gently pushed the corner of the receiving blanket off of his face and gazed down at him. He literally took my breath away. He was *beautiful*. That was the exact same thought I'd had when I'd first laid eyes on

Shard.

"Oh my god ..." I gently ran a fingertip down the middle of his forehead, over his nose, past his lips, and over the little dimple in his perfect chin—the same dimple that was in my chin.

"I told you," said Camille with an adoring smile as she leaned over to nuzzle her nose over his soft cheek. "He's even more beautiful than you were as a baby. He looks like you *and* Shard." She studied him closer. "He's got your chin. But he's got Shard's nose and mouth ... and *definitely* his eyes."

I nodded in agreement. My baby certainly had those deep, sharp, dark eyes. Camille removed his hat, and I gasped to see that his head was crowned with luscious, glossy black curls.

I carefully moved the blanket from the baby's body and counted his fingers. Then I counted his toes. Everything was perfect and all there.

"He's just so small," I fretted. "Is he gonna be okay like this?"

"Oh, it's common for preemies to weigh a little below the average size of a full-termer," said the nurse, quickly dismissing my worries with a wave of her hand. "You'll be surprised at how quickly he'll start to grow. He's actually quite large for a baby born in the seventh month." She gave me a questioning look. "Have you thought about what you're going to name him?"

At that moment, I realized that I hadn't given my child's name any serious thought at all. I momentarily considered naming him after Shard, but suddenly recalled Shard once telling me that in some circles, his name meant "strong ruler."

"If your daddy's the king, that would make you the little prince, huh?" I said to the baby. "Maybe I'll call you Prince."

Camille frowned. "Prince? Like the singer?"

"No, Prince like *royalty*."

"Well, why don't you change it up just a little bit? How about '*Princeton*'? You can call him 'Prince' for short, if you want."

I started to protest, but realized that I actually liked the idea.

"Princeton Phaylon," I said, trying the name out. I grinned at him. "That's an important-sounding name for such a tiny little thing. I hope you live it to up."

Camille bought a car seat so that Prince could leave the hospital with me two days later. The doctors had wanted to make sure that my pressure was stabilized before they would release me and the baby. I kept thinking about all of the things that I had purchased for Prince just months before he was born. There had been so many necessities. I didn't want to depend on my family to take care of me and my child. I really wanted to go back to Chesterfield, go into the house, and get the stuff; but I wanted to be sure that it was okay first.

The only problem was that I didn't have any way of contacting Shard. He didn't even know that I had given birth. I didn't have a number or anything else for him. Not even an address that would enable me to write. All I could do was wait for him to call me. I expected to hear from him pretty soon, because he had seemed to develop a time pattern for asking for his money. It was usually about every ten days or so—just a little under two weeks at a time.

When I got home, I had no choice but to take maternity leave from school. I was exhausted, and I slept a lot. Granny and Jazz took alternating days off from work in order to stay with me and help take care of the baby. Everyone was smitten with Prince. Somebody was always holding him, or talking and cooing to him as they walked around the house, rocking him in their arms. He became ridiculously spoiled—so much so that he screamed something awful whenever anyone tried to lay him down. Camille pleaded with me to let her go out and buy everything that he needed. I refused her offer, though, and I swore to her that if she went out and made any major purchases, I wouldn't use them. I assured her that I had already bought the essentials. I just had to go and retrieve them. I did, however, allow her to buy T-shirts, diapers, bottles, pacifiers, and a few toiletries for him.

I had helped to take care of Will when he had been a baby, so I could remember a few things like changing diapers, bathing, and dressing. I had to learn so many other things at one time in order to care for my newborn, though. I had to be taught how to heat his bottles, and then test his formula to be sure that it wasn't too hot. I had to learn how to firmly but gently pat his back to release the trapped air in his little belly. I had to learn how to clean the area inside of his belly button where a piece of the umbilical cord remained. It was a big job; but every time I looked at him, I was more than happy to do it. I realized more every day that he and I would be a constant part of each other for the rest of our lives. That was the only thing in my life that was absolutely certain, and that was enough for me.

Exactly seven days after Prince and I had come home from the hospital, I was sitting on my bed feeding him when I heard the phone ring. A few seconds later, Will headed into my room with the cordless extension in his hand.

"Telephone, Kyla."

I took the receiver from him, and then propped it between my ear and shoulder blade. "Hello?"

"What's up? What you doing?"

I dropped the bottle from Prince's mouth as I realized that it was Shard on the other end. Immediately, Prince began to whine and fuss, preparing to let out one of his notorious screams. I frantically reached for the bottle, all the while still balancing him and the phone. By the time I had grabbed the bottle from the mattress, he was wailing as loud as a siren. I slid the nipple back into his mouth and gently rolled it around to let him know that it was there. His lips locked around it, and he was instantly silenced.

"Hello?" I said into the receiver. "Are you still there?" There was silence on the other end. I thought that Shard had hung up, or that I had accidentally disconnected the call. "Hello?"

Shard finally spoke. "I'm still here. Whose baby you got over there?"

"Yours."

He chuckled sarcastically. "Yeah, right."

"I'm serious. He was premature. I went into labor on the 12th."

"Stop playing, Kyla."

"I'm for real. Why would I play about something like that? He's nine days old. You can ask my granny if you don't believe me. Ask anybody."

"You're serious?" He sounded bewildered. "How could you have it so early? Is that normal? Is that healthy?"

"He's fine now. We both are. The doctors said that my pressure was too high, and that's probably why he came early." There was a heavy silence, and I knew that Shard was thinking about my overdose. I knew that he was blaming me for our son's premature delivery.

"So it's a 'he'? It's a boy?"

"Yeah." I smiled. "He looks so much like you. Everybody says so."

"Man, I knew it was gonna be a boy. The way that kid was kicking ... *Had* to be a boy. So what's his name?"

"Princeton. We call him 'Prince'."

"Prince?" he repeated. "Any particular reason why you didn't name him after me?"

"I just thought that Prince fit him. I made 'Rashard' his middle name, though."

"I guess that's cool. So he's a good-looking kid? He looks healthy and happy and all that?"

"Yeah. He's been steadily gaining weight since we left the hospital. He was exactly 4 pounds at birth. Now he's already 4 pounds and 12 ounces. Almost 5 pounds. He has your eyes, too."

"Does he?"

"He even has your skin complexion. That real pretty caramel color. He also has your nose and mouth. And he's got the prettiest hair ever." I gently brushed my fingertips through the baby's curly black mane.

"So what does he look like inside of the diaper?" asked Shard seriously.

"What?"

"You know what I'm talking about. What is he working with in that area? He look like his daddy down there?"

I rolled my eyes. "He's just a baby. You should be insulted if anybody ever tells you that your nine-day-old son has one like yours. That would mean that something is *really* wrong with your body."

"Or that something is really *right* with his."

I tossed my head back and laughed. "You are so crazy."

My smile suddenly faded, though, and my eyes flooded with warm, salty water. Why did I have to sit on a phone and describe my baby to his father? We were sharing our firstborn son, yet we couldn't be together. It didn't seem fair. I sniffled, and Shard was silent for a moment. I knew that he could sense my pain.

"You ah-ight?" he asked.

"No. It's not supposed to be like this, Shard." The tears dripped from my eyes and splattered onto the front of Prince's T-shirt. I couldn't really explain, but I knew that Shard understood my point.

"It won't be this way forever," he said softly. "We just have to be patient."

"I know." I leaned down and kissed my baby's forehead. Surprisingly, it made me feel a little better. I dried my tears, wanting to change the subject. "I need to get into the house," I told Shard as I suddenly remembered the other reason that I had been awaiting his call.

"Why?"

"Because I left all of the stuff that I bought for the baby in one of the spare bedrooms."

"You can't go over there, Kyla. You already know the situation. You can't touch the house or the cars or anything. Don't even go to Chesterfield, ah-ight?"

"What am I supposed to do about getting all the things that Prince needs? There was a crib in there, and a stroller, and a swing, and a bunch of other stuff. He's here now. I can't keep putting it off."

"About a thousand dollars should cover it all, right? Take it out of the account and go get new stuff. Just don't go back to the house."

"I have to do something different with your money, too. My aunt found out that Nina was taking care of it, and she flipped out about it."

"Who gives a damn? Your cousin is over twenty-one, right? What the hell does her mother have to do with this?"

"I just don't want to put a strain on their relationship," I explained. "If she doesn't feel comfortable with us involving Nina, then I don't think that we should."

"Oh, so that's how you're gonna do me? Even though you know how much I need this, you're gonna let them tricks influence you to fuck up everything that I'm trying to accomplish?"

"What are you talking about? Nobody's influencing me to do anything. I just want to find some other way to go about this. It's not fair to involve them if they aren't feeling it. She's worried about the money and how you got it. She just doesn't want her daughter's name attached to something that might come back to get her later on."

"So she's worried about the way a man made his money, huh?" Shard scoffed. "That's a first for one of those scandalous-ass broads."

"Why do you have to keep disrespecting my family like that, Shard?"

"Oh. My fault. I'm the bad guy here. I'm down here trying to find a way to get my money discreetly so that I can provide a legit life for you and my kid, but I'm the enemy, right? Do you even know why I need the money transferred bit by bit to me? It's so that I can pay rent and utilities in this cramped-ass spot that I'm living in. I'm going to work every day with Mal, busting my ass on a loading dock just so I can make enough change to buy other shit like groceries after I get the money that you send me.

"I'm trying to spend as little as I can of what's in the bank so that there'll be something left for us when you get here. I'm going through all of this while you're telling me that your aunt is worried about how I got my money? You tell your aunt I said she can kiss my ass, ah-ight? And I'll tell you what *you* can do. Just withdraw all my shit and wire it to me through the same account that you send all the other withdrawals. You do that for me, and I won't ask you to do nothing else, ah-ight?"

"Wait." I could sense that he was about to hang up. "You know I don't mind doing things for you. Why are you getting so pissed at me?" He didn't respond. "Why didn't you tell me before about the way things are going with you? I didn't know that it was quite that bad."

"Yeah, well, that was the main reason why I didn't want to bring you here with me," he mumbled. "Ever since we been together, I've been able to give you the type of life that most women can only dream about. Cars, clothes, jewelry, a big house... Now that I'm living hand to mouth, I can't even provide you with half of that. Hell, I couldn't give you a third of it. If I can't give you all that anymore, then what's to stop you from leaving?"

"How many times do I have to tell you that it's not the money that I love, Shard? It's you. All I care about is us being a family and making a home for Prince. I care about having someone who can be a good man to me and a good father to him. I'm telling you, baby, once you lay your eyes on him, your life won't ever be the same again. He really puts things into perspective. All this stuff that we've been stressing ourselves and each other about ... it all seems so small in comparison."

I looked down at the baby again. He had fallen asleep in my arms. His face was absolutely angelic.

Shard was unenthusiastic. "Maybe. Look, just take the grand to get what you need and go ahead and send me the rest so I can get out of your hair. I don't want to be a burden to you."

"I never said you were a burden. Why are you acting like this?"

My ear was assaulted by a loud click, and then the dial tone. He had hung up. I sat there for several seconds, just holding the phone, stunned, until the loud recording came through the speaker, advising me to hang up. I pressed the button to turn the receiver off. Then I gently pulled the bottle from Prince's mouth. He didn't stir. I held him closer to my chest and savored his warmth. His sweet, baby-soft aroma drifted up and caressed my nostrils. He was an instant relaxant.

"I'm so glad I have you," I purred at him. "No matter what goes wrong now, one look at you makes everything okay."

After a few minutes, I laid him down on the baby blanket that I had spread on top of my comforter. Then I reached up for the small stereo on the shelf over the bed and turned the volume up just a notch. Soft music seemed to help him sleep through the night.

I stared down at the phone, wondering if Shard was going to call back. I knew him well enough to know that he wouldn't, though—at least not this night.

I walked over to the dresser against the far wall and gazed at my reflection in the mirror as I gathered the tail of my shirt in my hands and pulled it up. I inspected my midsection from the front, and then I turned and examined it from the side. After pinching the inch of extra flesh that had formed there since my pregnancy, I guesstimated that a month of vigorous diet and exercise would sculpt my body back into the hourglass silhouette it had formerly had.

I turned slowly and zeroed in on every square inch of skin. My hips, which had been voluptuous since my teens, now curved even deeper than an interstate highway. My butt was rounder than a plump, ripe, Georgia peach, and my thighs were thicker than molasses. I still had the body of a vixen and a face prettier than the roses on the bushes in Granny's backyard.

I also had more business savvy than some of the capitalists on Wall Street. More intellect than some of the fools on Easy Street. I could be as abrasive as sandpaper or as smooth as silk. Hard as a rock or as soft as a marshmallow. I had been as ferocious as a lioness when Shard needed me to be, and as meek as a lamb when he wanted me to be.

Even with all of that to my credit, I was still chasing this man to the ends of the earth and back again. A man who was no more mine *this* day than he had been three years earlier. A man who seemed farther away from me in spirit and soul than he was in meters and miles.

And knowing all this deep inside of myself, I still stood there ... gazing into that mirror and trying to figure out what it was that I kept doing wrong—or couldn't do right. I wondered why nothing that I did ever seemed to satisfy him.

Six

I didn't want Shard to think that I had been unwilling to continue helping him. But he had asked me to wire the rest of his money, so that was what I told Nina to do. Over a period of several weeks, she funneled the money in small amounts to the account in Jacksonville until there wasn't a cent of it left in St. Louis. Though I wasn't happy about the way that Shard and I ended our last conversation, I was relieved that Denise wouldn't have to worry about Nina's involvement with the money anymore. Denise and I had come to a silent truce about everything, just as Jazz and I had. We never mentioned our argument again.

I went out and bought the things that Prince needed after everything had been squared away. That was a big relief for me because I didn't want my baby to have to go without anything. I kept feeling this overwhelming sense of guilt after Shard had told me about the way that he was struggling, though. I lay awake a lot of nights, thinking of him working himself ragged. Though I didn't want him to feel unhappy or unsatisfied, I had to admit that I was glad that he was holding an honest job. It gave me hope that he and I could make a normal life for our baby. I didn't care if we had to struggle for a while, as long as we struggled together.

I couldn't wait for him to contact me so that I could tell him that. I had been almost certain that he would feel remorseful for the way that we had parted and that he would call me back to make amends. But a week later I still had heard nothing from him. I started to worry about his life in Florida. I wondered if he was seeing other women. I wondered if he was being as unfaithful to me there as he had been at home. I convinced myself, though, that because he was working so hard, he didn't have time to mess around.

While he was in Florida working to eat, his son was in Missouri getting as fat as a little suckling pig. Everything that the doctors and nurses at the hospital had told me was quickly coming to fruition. Prince's appetite seemed to double by the week. Before I knew it, he was downing a full bottle of formula in less than forty-five minutes. By the time he was a month old, he looked like a beached baby whale when he was laid out in his crib. He started developing rolls of fat underneath his chin, around his arms, on his thighs, and around his ankles. The fat around his arms even caused dimples at his elbows.

As Prince was gaining weight, I was eating yogurt, cottage cheese, and fruit so that I could *lose* weight. I ran around the track at one of the local high schools for an hour every day, and then did two hundred crunches as soon as I finished. It wasn't long at all before the little rolls of flesh on my belly disappeared and tightened into lean, taut muscle. The only parts of my body that jiggled a little were the parts that made men drool. The parts that looked like they had been liquefied, and then poured into my blouses and skirts.

A lot of the guys started to get bold when they saw me out, because they believed one of the many rumors that had started circulating about Shard. There were rumors that he had been arrested and was doing ten to fifteen years in prison. Rumors that he had fled the country and was lying up on a beach somewhere in Antigua. Rumors that he had gone incognito to Mexico and was doing migrant work to survive. Nina told me that she had even heard that his father had connections with a powerful mafia family, and that Shard was living in Sicily, in the lap of Italian luxury.

All of the rumors were ridiculous to me, of course, but people had no other way to explain his sudden disappearance. And when people didn't have answers, they made assumptions. They invented theories, which they spread as truth. That was just human nature.

Because of all of that, though, I had to deal with so many guys approaching me. So many guys coming out of the woodwork to tell me that they wanted to be with me. These guys told me that they would never walk out on me like Shard had. Some of them were kind of sweet, even in their insensitivity. The women were a different story entirely. They gave me these superior looks and made really snide remarks in my presence. If I went out and ran into girls from the north side or from East, they would walk up to me with smiles painted on their faces.

"Hey, Kyla," they would say, "I heard you had your baby. Everybody says that he is *so* cute." And then after I thanked them for the compliment, they would slyly add something like, "So how is Shard doing, girl? Have you even heard from him? That nigga know he was wrong for leaving you by yourself with a baby like that."

All this phony-ass concern for me and my child. I knew that they were rejoicing deep inside. Hell, some of them could barely keep from smiling while they were talking to me!

One weekend, Nina and I headed out to a shoe store called Pathways. A girl from East named Teresa was working there. She was on a stepladder stacking boxes on the top shelf when we walked in. She did a double take when she saw me, but pretended to be engrossed in her work. Olivia, another girl from the east side, was the store manager. She appeared to be taking stock inventory, but she gave Teresa *the look*. Soon, the two of them had disappeared to the rear of the store. I paid them no mind. While Nina sat on a stool to try on a pair of heels, I wandered over to the children's shoes to find a pair of baby sneakers for Prince. As I browsed the infants' aisle, I heard soft female voices drifting from the other side. I totally disregarded the muffled conversation until I heard my name,

"*Kyla.*"

I leaned forward so that I could hear what was being said about me and frowned.

"*Girl, you know that she ain't got shit now that he's gone. He had her rolling in that BMW and coming to the east-side in chinchilla coats and shit. That's why I ain't never liked her. She thought she was all that because she was with him.*"

"*I know, girl. I mean, she's cute, but he was still cheating on her. I guess she wasn't handling her business the way she should have been.*"

"*I guess not. She was out trying to fight every girl that looked at him; and that still didn't stop him from doing what he wanted to do. Now she's sitting up here, rocking his baby, while he gone somewhere doing his own thing. I knew it wouldn't be too long before he dropped her ass. That girl is dumb as hell if she thought that baby was gonna lock him down.*"

I heard the two voices chuckle softly. Angry, I just turned and walked briskly back to the other side of the store, where Nina was walking around in the shoes that she had just put on.

"What you think about these?" she asked as she saw me returning. "Should I get 'em?"

I ignored her question. "Let's go."

"What's wrong with you?"

"Nothing. I'm just ready to go. Let's get the hell outta here."

"Well, damn. Can I pay for the shoes first?"

She sat back down on the stool to remove the heels and

place them back into the box. I stood over her and folded my arms over my chest. A few seconds later, I saw Teresa and Olivia walking down our aisle. They both had strange smirks on their faces. I realized that it had been the two of them that I had overheard.

"Hey," they chorused with smiles and waves as they passed me and Nina. "How y'all doing?"

"Hey," Nina greeted them.

I just rolled my eyes and sneered. "I can't *stand* these bitches around here," I told Nina as I glared at their backs. I spoke loudly enough to be sure that they had heard me. "Always in somebody's business." Both girls turned to look at me, expressions of surprise on their faces. I raised an eyebrow and gave them a "Yeah-I'm-talking-about-you" look. They didn't respond, though. They just turned and kept walking.

"What are you talking about?" asked Nina as she stood with her shoe box in hand and grabbed her purse from the stool.

"Forget it. Go ahead and pay for your shoes. I'll wait for you outside."

I had never been easily hurt by other people's words, but the scathing nature of those comments had cut me deeply. Coincidentally, Shard called me that very night. It had been three weeks since I had spoken to him. Our chat started out rather dry because of the bitter note on which our last conversation had ended.

When he asked about Prince, I took the time to catch him up on everything that he had missed the past few weeks.

The way that Prince had begun to make cute little gurgling noises whenever I kissed his belly. The way that he was focusing his eyes on everything that entered his line of vision. Shard seemed to be only half-listening to me, though. It was obvious that he was preoccupied with something else. I decided to cut through the small talk.

"So when are you coming to get us?" I blurted out.

"Kyla, don't start this. I told you the situation already. I shouldn't have to keep explaining shit to you. You only put more pressure on me when you do this."

"No, Shard, the pressure's on *me*. I'm the one who's having to sit here and listen to these silly-ass girls around here talking all this mess about us. It's been two months already. I mean, why can't you just send for me and Prince? I don't have to finish school right now. I'll get a job, and I'll help you pay bills. Even if I have to clean houses ... scrub floors ... whatever. I don't care. Just please let me come and be with you."

"Not now."

My voice broke with tears. "I'm *begging* you."

He was unmoved by my show of emotion. "*No*, Kyla."

"Why do you want me to stay here and put up with this?" My thoughts automatically went back to the things that the girls in the store had said. "I thought you loved me."

"You're so damn selfish," he declared. "All you keep talking about is yourself and what you're going through. You think all this is easy for me? You think I like lying in bed every night, knowing that any day now, the bank is gonna foreclose on my house, and the repo-man is gonna come and tow my cars away? That's the type of shit *I'm* having to deal with. So don't come at me with a sob story about some gossiping broads that hurt your feelings. You better grow a backbone."

I sniffled as I stared down at my hands and watched the teardrops rain from my eyes.

"You know what," he said irritably, "I ain't even got the energy for waterworks tonight. Every time I talk to you, it's the same bullshit and drama. All you do is stress me out." He sighed loudly. "I'll tell you what. I'm gonna give you some more time to get yourself together. The next time I call, you need to come correct. If you don't think you can do that, then just don't answer the phone, ah-ight?"

I was silent. *He's right,* I told myself. *I'm overreacting, and I'm stressing him.*

"You understand that?" he asked.

"Yeah, I understand."

After Shard and I hung up, I realized that I *had* been selfish. I knew how hard he was working in Florida. I could only imagine how difficult it must have been to have to start life all over in a strange place, surrounded by strange people. He basically had to start from scratch; and instead of support-ing and encouraging him, I was only nagging and riding him about my petty concerns. I should have been praising him at every opportunity. I should have been telling him how proud I was of him for finally making an honest man of himself. After that last conversation, he started to call even less frequently. I decided to go out and get a job so that I could take care of Prince's needs. I had promised myself that I wouldn't put any more financial pressures on Shard. In fact, I decided I would stop putting *any* type of pressure on him, period.

That was why I started to keep all of my problems hidden whenever we did speak. I no longer shared my fears, my worries, my sadness, or my pain with him. I tried to fake my happiness. Sometimes I would be sitting there, holding the phone to my ear with fat tears standing in my eyes while I lied and told him how well things were going for me. The truth was, I was miserable; but I knew he was miserable, too, so I lied in order to spare him.

The only person with whom I shared my true feelings was my son. I would lie in bed next to him, with my hand on his head, just talking to him while I held his bottle in his mouth. I told him everything. I mean, I spoke to him as if he could understand every word that I uttered.

He had Shard's deep, soulful, dark eyes, so it seemed that he comprehended everything that I said. In him, physically, I saw a lot of Shard. Spiritually, though, I saw myself. You could call it a bond between a mother and her child; but I definitely felt a type of connection with him that I had never felt with any other human being. If it hadn't been for Prince, I surely would have fallen into another severe bout of depression. He was the only thing that kept me going. He became my reason for dragging my wretched soul out of bed every morning and facing the day. He became my reason for silently tolerating all of the hurtful, thoughtless things that people said to me. I was strong for him, when I couldn't be strong for myself.

Prince was also the main reason why I set out to find

some work. I lucked up by finding a job opening for a secretary at a construction company in the classified section of the newspaper. I went down to put in an application, and I was actually interviewed the same day. Two days later, I got a phone call offering me the job. I was expected to bring some organization to the office. I did a lot of sorting, typing, and filing. My boss was a white man in his fifties named Bill. He had a big beer belly; and even though he wore a belt in the loop of his jeans, they always looked as if they were about to fall off his butt. He walked around with the top two buttons on his flannel shirt undone, and his white foreman's hat was a perpetual part of his attire. The man was a walking cliché.

Bill was always nice to me, very respectable and professional. The other guys, though, were a completely different story for a while. My first week on the job, I was subjected to catcalls, whistles, and a few other declarations of their physical attraction to me. When I walked out onto the site dressed in the white linen blouse and short black skirt that I had gotten from Jazz, or the pin-striped hip-huggers and matching blazer that I had left at home two years earlier, they would all yell and hoot like jungle animals.

It wasn't until Bill appealed to them on my behalf that they all began to show more respect. They would nod politely and say "good morning," but as soon as I walked by, I would feel a hundred pair of eyes watching my hips and backside until I disappeared inside of the air-conditioned trailer that housed the office.

The pay was just a little over minimum wage, but the

work was steady. It felt good to be able to go into my own purse and purchase things for my son. I didn't have to constantly stick my hand out in front of Granny's face to request money for a package of diapers, a few cans of formula, or a bottle of baby oil. She never complained, though. In fact, she had often come to me just to ask me if I needed anything for the baby. When Jazz was planning a trip to the store, she would also stick her head in my bedroom and ask if there was anything that she could bring back. Despite their willingness to help, though, I just didn't feel comfortable spending so much of their money.

Camille sent me a four-hundred dollar check every month to start a college fund for Prince. It was kind of strange the way that Camille latched onto the baby from the very beginning. It seemed that she was more enamored by him than she had *ever* been by me. She called every other day to inquire about him. She even sent me an extra two hundred dollars when he was almost two months old, and told me to take him down to a studio and have some pictures taken of him. At the end of every month, I would go down to the post office to find that she had sent a cardboard box, packed with at least three adorable baby outfits, a pair of shoes, and sometimes, some type of accessory like a hat or a jacket.

The older Prince got, the more handsome he became. When I took him out in his stroller, *everybody* would walk over and make a fuss about him.

"Ooh, would you look at this ba-by!" women in the grocery store would coo. "He is just gorgeous!" Men would even look down at him and say things like, "That's a real cute kid."

I didn't mind things like that. The only thing that bothered me was when women just walked up and reached down into the stroller uttering, "Aww ... can I hold him?" I was very overprotective, so I would cringe and grip the handles of the stroller tightly while I watched them gently cradle him and purr over his adorableness. Then, after about three seconds, I would start reaching out in a "give-me-back-my-baby" gesture.

I paid Will's babysitter, Ms. Prescott, to watch Prince. Every weekday morning, I woke up extra early to push his stroller to Ms. Prescott's house. Then, I walked to the bus stop and waited for the seven-fifteen bus, so that I could arrive at work a little before eight. I worked hard all day long, and then at four thirty, I rode the bus back home and walked to Ms. Prescott's to pick up both Will and Prince.

Once we arrived home, I would place Prince in his mechanical swing in the living room. Then, I would change into some comfortable clothes, and while Will did his homework, I would wash the dishes and start dinner. After Will and I had eaten, I would bathe and then spend the remainder of the evening calming my fussy baby, changing his diapers, and entertaining him. By ten, I would fall out across my bed and sleep until either a screaming Prince or my screaming alarm clock would wake me up at five forty-five the next morning to start the routine again.

At twenty years old, that was the story of my life. All work and no play. It wasn't long before I was exhausted, but I reminded myself that I was an adult. Adults had to work to survive. Plus, I was a mother. That meant that I had somebody who depended on me for everything. *Everything*. No matter how tired I got, that thought always energized me.

Not knowing how to contact Shard was very difficult for me, though. I no longer had a cell phone because I had wanted to cut down on my bills, so I had to wait to receive his calls on Granny's house phone. He always seemed to know exactly when to call, too, because he always managed to catch me before I left the house or after I had just returned to it.

I could never retrieve his number from the Caller ID display. It was always blocked. I didn't know anything about the telephone system, but I figured that by blocking his phone number, Shard was taking an extra precaution to be sure that his calls were never traced. That was why I didn't ask him to give me a contact number. I didn't know if other ears were listening to us. I didn't hear from him during the *entire* month of April. He didn't even call to check on Prince. I started to worry. His phone calls had always been few and far between, but he had never gone an entire month without reaching me.

It was a very warm Sunday in early May when I got the most unexpected phone call I had ever received. I was sitting on the back steps underneath the shade of the awning over the door with my baby on my lap. He was propped against my chest, and I was pointing out objects in the backyard to him. He was so alert for such a young child. I was trying to take advantage of that by developing his recognition skills early on.

"Look, Prince," I cooed in a singsongy voice as I pointed at a sparrow that had landed on the fence across the way.

"That's a birdy. You see the birdy, baby?" I looked down at him, and laughed as he drooled and rolled his head back against my bosom. I gently wiped his mouth and chin with the bib that was tied loosely around his neck. Just as I finished, I heard the phone ringing inside the kitchen.

I gathered Prince in my arms and stood up. "Why didn't you remind me to bring the cordless out here?" I said to him. "Why didn't you remind Mommy?" I pulled the screen door open and headed inside the kitchen.

"How come you didn't answer the phone, Will?" I fussed as my cousin skirted around the kitchen door and headed for the refrigerator while I lifted the receiver from the wall extension and balanced Prince in my free arm.

"Hello?"

There was silence.

"Hello?" I repeated. There was a short click, and then a flush of sound as a recorded male voice boomed through the speaker.

"This call is from a Missouri state correctional institution. Please be informed that your call will be monitored and recorded. Will you accept charges?"

I swallowed hard and held my baby tighter. I suddenly felt weak in the knees.

Shard is in jail, I thought. *They arrested him.*

"Y-yes," I said shakily into the phone. "I'll accept." I gripped the receiver as I waited to hear his greeting. There was another click, and then I heard a bit of noise in the background.

"Hello?" I had to lean back against the wall for support.

"Yes? Hello?" came a smooth male voice. It *almost* sounded like Shard—but not quite. There was a heavier air of maturity to this particular voice. A somberness that I had never heard in Shard's voice.

I frowned in confusion. "Shard?" I said softly.

"No. This isn't Rashard. Might I be speaking with Ms. Kyla Brown?"

"Yeah. This is Kyla. Who's this?"

"We've never met. I'm Maxwell Phaylon. I'm Rashard's father."

I was so taken aback by his introduction, I had to pull one of the chairs out from underneath the table and sit down.

"Hi." I suddenly felt shy. "How are you?"

"I'm fine, and you?"

"Good."

"I hope I'm not too far out of line by contacting you. But I really needed to speak with you."

"With *me*?"

"Yes. I need to see you. In person."

"What do you need?"

"Just a little bit of your time. I'm at Algoa, in Jefferson City. It's only about two and a half hours from St. Louis. Can you come?"

I was hesitant. I had no idea how Shard's father had gotten my phone number. I didn't know why he needed me to come to the prison. What was going on? The question wasn't being answered in my head, so I decided to verbalize it.

"What is it that you need from me?"

He refused to reveal any information. "All I need is for you to come here as soon as possible. Can you do that for me?"

I didn't want to deny his request. If he had taken the pains to locate me and then call me, he must have really needed me for some reason.

"Yes. I'll come."

He seemed satisfied. "Thank you, I'll see you soon."

Seven

I had never been to a prison to visit anyone.

       I didn't know what to expect when I borrowed my Granny's car the next Thursday to drive to Jefferson City. Everything that I thought I knew about prison visits I had learned by watching TV and movies. I expected to go into a room and sit down at a counter facing a window. Then, I imagined that Shard's father would be escorted into the room in handcuffs and shackles. A guard would lead him to a stool on the other side of the counter, and he would sit down, facing me with the thick, impenetrable glass between the two of us. Finally, we would have to lift the telephone receiver that we each had within our reach and communicate with one another through the mouthpiece.

Right outside of the prison grounds, a shuttle bus picked up a group of visitors, including myself. My heart thudded out of my chest when I boarded the white bus with the visitors. I tried not to stare at the other passengers on the bus, but I couldn't help but notice how different we all looked. We seemed to have come from all walks of life. There were blacks, whites, and Hispanics. There were men, women, and a couple of children. Teenagers, adults, and a few senior citizens. We were all as diverse as humanly possible, yet we had one thing in common. We were all connected in one way or another to some soul that had been captured and removed from the world of which we were a part. Some soul that no longer enjoyed the most basic and essential human right: freedom.

I gazed out the window, watching the large prison complex that loomed ahead grow larger as the bus narrowed the distance that separated me from it. Visiting an inmate was more of a process than I had thought. There were procedures that had been put in place to insure that no undesirable activity occurred within the walls of the complex.

Of course, I had to remove all of my jewelry before I even got past the entrance. I eyed the uniformed male guard with contempt as he licked his lips longingly, and his eyes fell to my waist, past my hips, and then up to my face. He waved his hand-held metal detector *very* slowly down my front. Then he walked around me and waved it even slower down the back of my body. I could feel those eyes of his following the path of the detector.

After I passed the inspection, there were papers that had to be signed. I had arrived there at eight thirty am, and it was nine thirty before I even sat down in the large visiting room. I chose a round table with two orange plastic chairs and sat down to wait. While I waited, I watched all of the activity around me. Mothers tearfully hugged their sons, kids playfully ran up to their fathers. Wives and girlfriends kissed their men hello. I could only imagine what my life would be like if I had to come to a place like that to visit a loved one of my own.

I watched the desolate-looking men as they wobbled over to their visitors, their normal gaits interrupted by the metal chains that held their ankles close together. Most of them wore their prison jumpsuits like badges of shame. It was a sad sight.

I tried to mentally prepare myself for Mr. Phaylon. I took several deep breaths as I watched the door that had delivered all of the other inmates to the room. I tried to imagine what he would look like. Would he look worn and tired from years of hard prison life? Would he, too, wobble into the room with his head hung low and his spine bent in submission? I nervously drummed my fingernails over the surface of the small table. After several minutes, I began to wonder if Mr. Phaylon had even been informed that I was there for him. Maybe I had not gone through every step of the procedure. Maybe there were other papers that I needed to sign. I rose to my feet and turned to walk over to the guard who stood against the wall at the east entrance of the room. That was when the east entrance door slowly opened.

And *he* walked in.

I didn't have to wonder who he was. I didn't doubt his identity for even a split second. I swallowed hard as I watched his dark eyes search the room. As soon as those eyes landed on me, his mouth turned up into a tiny smile at each corner. He navigated through the sea of people and maze of tables with incredible agility. His movements were effortless. His stride was confident. His gait was graceful. He almost looked as if he were floating toward me instead of merely walking. I looked down at his feet and noticed that he wore no shackles.

His hands were not cuffed. In fact, he didn't even wear a jumpsuit. He was dressed in a light blue button-down shirt and navy blue slacks that were belted neatly at the waist. The other inmates stepped aside as he walked past. I saw the gazes of respect and deference that they laid upon him as he sauntered over to me. When we were standing less than one foot apart, he placed his hands behind his back and watched me. His steady gaze intimidated me. My eyes fell from his and rested somewhere around his neck area.

"Kyla." He said my name with absolute certainty.

"Hi," I said shyly.

He reached out and placed a hand under my chin, then firmly lifted it. "We can't have a proper conversation if you don't look at me. How would I know that I can trust you if we can't even make eye contact?"

I looked into those oh-so-familiar eyes of his. "I'm sorry. It's just that ... you look just like him. I mean ... *he* looks just like *you*. And my baby. You all look so much alike ..."

"Your baby," repeated Mr. Phaylon. "Yes. I had gotten word that I have a grandson now. How old is he?"

"He just turned four months old."

"And you're sure that he's my grandchild? That isn't something that I would like to be deceived about."

"Yes." I was hurt by the question. "Shard is the only man I've been with in three years."

"That's what all you women say when you get knocked up." Mr. Phaylon circled the table and sat down. "You all swear that you only have one lover. Take a look around you, young lady. It's the same situation in here. Every man in this room swears that he's innocent of the crimes that he's being accused of. Nobody ever wants to admit that they're only human. Nobody wants to admit that they're capable of getting caught up."

I raised a defiant eyebrow at him. "Well, I'm not worried about getting 'caught up.' Shard *is* my child's father. Point blank. Period."

He waved toward the vacant seat that faced him. "Sit down."

"I'd rather not." I folded my arms over my ample chest. "I didn't drive all this way to be insulted, Mr. Phaylon."

"Please," he said as he pulled a cigar out of his shirt pocket, "call me Max."

"No. I think 'Mr. Phaylon' will suffice."

He stared at me as he stuck the cigar between his lips and produced a silver Zippo from the same pocket. As he lit his cigar, he was still watching me. I met his gaze without even blinking this time. He grinned as he blew the first stream of smoke out of his nostrils.

"I like you," he decided, nodding his head. "I like you a lot. I had heard that you were a feisty one." He pointed at the chair again. "Please, sit down."

I slowly pulled the chair out and lowered myself to a sitting position.

He gave my face a slow once-over. "You are *stunning*. That was why I knew you at first glance. I know my son, and I know him well. He has a weakness for beautiful women. I guess he got that from me. I always thought of myself as Superman, but a pretty face was my Kryptonite."

I smiled in spite of my anger. My eyes involuntarily swept over his flawless honey-colored skin, his chiseled cheekbones and sculpted jawline, those full lips and wavy jet-black hair. And those incomparable eyes. Shard's resemblance to him was remarkable.

"How did you know where to find me?" I asked.

"I always keep an ear to the streets," Mr. Phaylon replied as he took another puff of his cigar. "People here keep me informed. You'd be surprised by what I could find out by just walking around the yard and talking to the right people. There's always somebody coming through those doors from the old neighborhood who catches me up on things. Always somebody going back out who keeps me posted, too. I've heard a lot about you. I've heard that you'll go to bat for Shard quicker than most of the so-called men in the 'hood do. Although just by looking at you, that's impossible to tell. Pretty women don't usually like to get their hands dirty."

"Never judge a book by its cover. A lot of people wouldn't associate Shard with his way of life if they just went by the way that he looks. I know *I* never guessed it ..." I added softly as

I looked down at my hands.

"When was the last time you saw him?" asked Mr. Phaylon.

"December."

Mr. Phaylon nodded. He glanced casually over each of his shoulders. Then he returned his attention to me. He lowered his voice confidentially. "There was a reason why I called you here. I need you to deliver a message."

"To Shard?"

"Yes. I can't talk to him over these phone lines about certain things. I can't even send him a letter because they read my mail here. And I can't trust many people to handle the business between me and my son. But if he trusts you, then I trust you, too. So, please ... deliver the message for me."

"I don't know when I'll talk to him again. All I can do is wait for his call."

"You'll talk to him soon." Mr. Phaylon blew more smoke out of his nostrils. "You'll talk to him very soon." He glanced down at the watch that he wore on his left wrist. "My time's almost up."

He rose to his feet and pushed his chair underneath the table again. Was this the only reason that I had come to Jefferson City? To promise Mr. Phaylon that I would deliver some mysterious message? It seemed ridiculous to me.

As I stood, I noticed that he was walking around the table with his arms spread wide. "Give me a hug."

This confused me even more. Why did he want to hug me? We had known each other less than an hour. Still, I obliged him. I narrowed the gap between us and slipped my arms around his neck. His arms encircled my waist. As quick as lightning, I felt his palm slide down the left side of my ass. I jumped a little then pulled away. I frowned even deeper at him, searching his face for any signs of remorse for what he had done. His expression revealed nothing, though. He and Shard were so much alike, it was scary. When they didn't want anyone to read their thoughts, they made it impossible to penetrate their minds. Mr. Phaylon gave me a quick wink then grabbed his lighter from the table. He turned and began to stride away.

"Wait … Mr. Phaylon?" I was trying not to rouse too much attention. "You didn't give me the message." He just kept walking as if he didn't hear me. "Mr. Phaylon?"

It was no use, though. In four seconds flat, he had disappeared through the exit. I still didn't fully understand what had happened. As I boarded the shuttle bus again, I began to believe that the trip had been made in vain. I thought back to Mr. Phaylon's hand on my ass. Maybe it was my own intuition, but for no particular reason, I placed the palm of my hand on the spot where his had been. That was when I heard the rustle inside of my pocket. I slipped my hand into my back left pocket. There, I felt a slip of paper.

I quickly took my seat on the bus, which would take me back to Granny's car. Once I edged up against the window, I unfolded the small slip. It was a wrinkled scrap of notebook paper, not much bigger than a book of matches.

Written on it in tiny, precise letters were two words:

"Complete success."

Underneath the message was a phone number with a 786 area code. I quickly stuffed the note back into my pocket.

When I finally opened the front door at Granny's house, it was almost two in the afternoon. The house was very quiet. I headed straight to the kitchen, figuring that Jazz and Will would be in there with Prince. The kitchen was empty. I headed down the hallway and peered into Jazz's room. There, I saw her napping on her bed. Prince was lying next to her, stretched out on his belly. The nipple of his bottle was still stuck in his mouth, but he was sound asleep. I eased out of the doorway, then headed into my bedroom and silently closed the door behind me. I quickly retrieved the cordless phone from its base and then sat down on the floor next to the bed, removed the note from my pocket again, unfolded it, and then dialed the number that was scrawled on it. Who was I going to ask for? Was I simply supposed to read the note to whoever answered the call?

I waited apprehensively as the extension on the other end rang. Once ... Twice ...

On the third ring, the line clicked. "Yeah?"

My eyes grew wide as I recognized the voice immediately. "*Shard*?"

"Yeah. It's me."

"Oh my god. Why haven't you called me? Do you know how worried I've been about you? I been sitting up here damn near pulling my hair out!"

"I'm sorry. But I had my reasons."

"What reasons? What reasons could keep you from calling to check on me and your child for almost a month and a half?"

"We'll talk about all that another time. Listen, how did you get this number? Did you talk to my dad?"

"Yeah. I actually saw him. I went to Algoa this morning to visit him."

"You went to Algoa? By yourself?"

"He called me last week and asked me to come."

"Word? He had said that he was gonna send word to me through somebody that we could both trust. I never guessed he would contact you, though. So did he want you to tell me anything?"

"He gave me a note," I said as I looked down at the paper again. "All it says is 'complete success.'"

"*Perfect.*" I could hear the satisfaction and approval resonating throughout his voice. "That's the best news anybody's ever given me, baby girl. Thank you."

"I'm so confused. What is this all about, Shard? Tell me something."

"All you need to know right now is that I'm taking care of everything. I want you to catch a flight up here this weekend."

"What? Are you serious?"

"Yeah. I've been setting aside a little paper for a rainy day. I'll get you a plane ticket, and you can come on up."

"Shard!" I squealed excitedly as I hopped to my feet and began to pace the floor with renewed energy. "Baby, I'll start packing my stuff up tonight. It's too late to give my boss two weeks' notice, but a week should be okay, shouldn't it? I have to find a storage to put Prince's stuff in, too. How long is the flight from here to Miami? It's not too long for him, is it?"

I was babbling so fast that it took me a moment to realize that Shard was trying to get my attention. "Kyla? *Kyla!*"

"What?"

"You're getting ahead of yourself just a little bit."

"Why do you say that?"

"I didn't mean that you were coming to stay. I still have some loose ends to tie up, and having you and a baby up here wouldn't fit into the equation at this point."

"Prince isn't *a* baby, he's *our* baby. And if you don't want us there to stay, then why do you want us there, period?"

"Right now, I just want *you* here. I want to see you. In another couple of months, you'll probably be able to come back permanently and bring Prince with you."

"*Probably*? What do you mean, *probably*? You told me that I would only have to wait five or six months before I could come there. It's been almost six months, Shard. So what are you telling me now, I have to wait another two?"

"What I'm telling you is that I have some more loose ends to tie up. What, you don't want to see me if it's not gonna be on your terms?"

"You know I want to see you. I just …" My sentence trailed as I realized how selfish I must have sounded to him. As much as it pained me to do so, I agreed to take the trip to Miami without Prince.

I made sure that Granny and Jazz knew that I was flying to a "secret location" for the sole purpose of seeing Shard. I wanted everyone to see that he hadn't left me permanently. I wanted them to know that our separation had only been temporary. Now the time had almost come for us to be together again. I wanted to gloat. I wanted to rub it in everyone's faces. Hell, I wanted to shout it from the rooftops!

As planned, Shard booked me a flight for the very next weekend.

I sat down and tried to concoct a legitimate excuse for Bill about why I wouldn't be working next Thursday and Friday. I had spent an entire day wracking my brain. I had already taken the last Thursday off to go and see Shard's father, and I hadn't accumulated any vacation time. Finally, I had decided that the easiest way to get out of working was to just quit my job. So that was what I did. I rode the bus down to the construction site on Monday morning with determination burning in my eyes. As soon as I opened the door of the air-conditioned trailer, I came face-to-face with Bill.

"Ah," he breathed with a wide grin, "how you doing, Kyla?" He consulted his watch, and then looked at me again. "You're almost half an hour late. First time you ever been late since I hired you."

"I know." I walked up the last step and closed the door behind me to block all of the noise that was drifting in from outside. "Actually, I need to talk to you about something, Bill. Do you have a minute?"

"Ah-right." He walked over to his desk and perched atop it. He focused all of his attention on me. "What's on your mind?"

I clutched my purse strap tightly and took a deep breath. I hated to leave without even giving him two weeks' notice, but

Baby
126
Girl II

I felt that I had no other choice.

"First of all," I started, "I want to thank you for the opportunity that you gave me. I've really enjoyed working here. I couldn't have asked for a better boss. I really appreciate that."

Bill folded his arms over his chest. "Uh-oh. If I didn't know any better, I would say that this sounds like a quitting speech."

I chewed on my bottom lip and nodded. "It is. Something's come up, and I have to leave town."

Bill's eyebrows shot up. "Do you mind if I ask what that is?"

"Well, I'm moving," I informed him. "I'm moving out of state with my son's father in July. I have to go Thursday, though, to take care of some things before the permanent move."

"I see. Well, we'll sure miss you around here. You've done a great job with this place." He waved around the neat office. He looked back at me. "You are taking that cute kid of yours with you, aren't you?"

"Oh, yeah. Of course. He's never laid eyes on his daddy, so it's gonna be real special."

"His father's never seen him?"

I instantly regretted telling him my business. "No, he hasn't," I answered.

"Oh," Bill said, suddenly looking as if he understood. "His father must have been stationed overseas. Is he a soldier?"

"Yeah. Something like that."

Later that night, I sat on my bed feeding Prince as I rocked him to sleep.

"Close those eyes," I said gently as I looked down at him. "I know you're tired. You only slept for a half hour today." He continued to gaze up at me with those glittery, olive-black orbs of his.

"Don't look at me like that. You're making me feel bad for leaving. Four days really isn't *that* long. You'll be here with Ms. Prescott, and Granny, and Jazz and Will." He just gazed silently at me as he tugged on the nipple of his bottle with his mouth. His entire hand was wrapped tightly around my finger.

"I *have* to go, Prince. You don't know how long I been waiting for this. I miss your daddy so much. It wouldn't make sense for me to wait another two months to see him when I could see him in just a few days, would it?"

Of course, Prince said nothing. He just continued to watch me.

I don't know why I was having that particular conversation with my child. Deep down inside, though, I knew that I was really having that debate with myself. How responsible was I really being by leaving my four-month-old baby behind while I traveled to another state? I knew that my family would take good care of him, but I was his mother. Nobody could give him the kind of attention and affection that I could. Would he somehow be able to sense that I was gone away from him? Would he be able to sleep through the night if he didn't feel the warmth of my touch and the love that radiated from within me just for him?

I leaned over and placed three kisses on his soft, sweet-smelling skin—one on his forehead, and one on each of his cheeks. Then, I stretched him out on his stomach and gently rubbed his back for a few minutes. Once I was certain that he was asleep, I reached up to turn on the radio, making sure to keep the volume low, then I headed out of my bedroom in search of my grandmother. I found her in the kitchen, putting away the leftovers from dinner.

Folding my arms over my chest and leaning against the door frame, I said, "Granny?"

She turned to face me as she closed the oven door. "Hmm?"

"Don't forget to play some soft music for Prince when you put him to sleep at night, okay?"

Granny smiled, "I won't forget, Kyla." She walked over to the refrigerator with two plastic Tupperware containers in hand.

"And you won't forget to put that yellow stuffed rabbit thing on the other side of him, will you? That seems to help him sleep even better. And don't forget to put him in the bed with you, okay? Don't make him sleep in that crib. I think he gets lonely in there."

"Kyla. I'm not gonna forget anything, okay? You told me all this a thousand times, baby. I'm not gonna forget."

"Okay." I tried to think of any information that I had overlooked as I turned to walk away.

"Kyla?" called Granny.

"Yeah?" I turned again.

"If you think that you'll be worrying yourself about him, maybe you just shouldn't go …"

"You don't think I should?" I stuck my thumbnail in my

mouth and chewed.

Granny shrugged her shoulders as she raked leftover spaghetti from the pot into a large container. "You really moving with him in August?"

"Yes ma'am. I told you that I was. I've been telling y'all that ever since I moved back in here. What, you didn't believe me?"

"Shard is a lucky young man," she said, "to have a beautiful, intelligent young woman like you at his disposal ... Many girls would never run to a man who left them alone and pregnant. He's got it made, though. He can just walk in and out whenever he feels like it. He knows you'll always be there with those catcher's mitts on. Always there to catch whatever he throws." She shook her head as she placed the lid on the container. "He's a very lucky young man," she repeated.

"Why are you trying to criticize my relationship now? In the past five months, you hadn't said anything."

"Because in those five months, he hasn't been around. And in the past *four* months, I've seen a side of you that I've never seen before. Ever since you had that baby, you've been different, Kyla. You've been mature, strong, and *so* independent. You've become a woman."

"I've always been like that."

"No." She shook her head. "You thought that all of your strength lied in Shard; and you depended on him to make you *feel* like a woman. You depended on him to make you a complete person. But ever since Prince came along, you've had to put all your own wants aside. That really made you grow up. I just hate to see you throw all that away now that Shard has decided that he's ready to have you back in his life."

"Granny, I never left his life."

"Are you sure that you were ever even a part of it?"

"What do you mean?"

Granny shut the refrigerator door hard and then turned to face me completely. The look of anguish that she held on her face startled me.

"Kyla, something has gone wrong." She wrapped her hand over the back of the nearest chair and stared down at the surface of the kitchen table. "I've raised five girls, including you. Five girls that became five beautiful women. Somewhere along the way, though, *something* went wrong. It can't be a coincidence that all y'all run around here, looking for a man to validate you, and then looking lost and confused when you finally realize that no man on earth can do that for you if you can't do it for yourself.

"On the one hand, I got a daughter who got burned by a bad relationship twenty years ago. Now she hides behind her fancy degrees and big job titles, scared to look too hard at *any* man."

I knew that Granny was referring to my mother.

"On the other hand," she continued, "I got a daughter who's spent the better part of her adulthood with a married man who *still* won't leave his wife ..."

Monica.

"I've got a daughter who can't give her child her father's last name because he won't even claim her as his own."

Denise.

"And a daughter who's been drifting in and out of one meaningless relationship after another ever since she was fifteen years old. Now she's too bitter to let anybody love her."

Jazz.

"And you." Her gaze came to rest on me. "You've been trying so hard to be different from the rest of them; but you're not, Kyla. You took a different path, but you're still heading in the same damn direction."

I was incensed. "I'll *never* end up like any of y'all, Granny. Because whether you realize it or not, you're in the same boat with your daughters. You're the one who taught them that all life was about was using your looks and your body to get what you want from a man. You're the one who taught them that the most important things that a woman could have were credit cards and a purse full of money. *That's* where everything went wrong. They didn't seek out men with big hearts. They all sought out men with big bank accounts. I almost became just like them, but I got out in time. I'm not like any of y'all."

"I'm not gonna have you standing here telling me that I'm a bad mother," said Granny. "I did the best that I could." She leaned heavier on the chair, and I saw her eyes fill with water. She pulled the chair out and sat down weakly in it. I remained standing, totally befuddled by her sudden display. She seemed to be pulling her strength from somewhere deep within herself.

"Let me tell you a story. When I was sixteen years old, my daddy's old buddy, a man by the name of Carl Lerner, came into town for a few days on his way to a gig in Chicago. He was a guitar player in the same blues band that my daddy had played saxophone in before he married my momma." She paused to wipe the tears that had belatedly fallen from her eyes.

"Carl showed up at our door one night with nothing but a guitar case and a smile, asking my daddy to let him stay with us until the rest of the band came through St. Louis to pick him up at the end of the week. My daddy welcomed him." She shook her head, and her eyes took on a faraway look.

"Carl had a look ... a way about him that made you just want to catch him and keep him locked up inside of you. He was so handsome, it almost hurt to look at him—just like Shard. Before the sun hit the sky the next morning, I was head over heels in love with that man. He didn't have a pot to piss in or a window to throw it out of, but I didn't care. I saw the way he looked at me, and I knew that he could sense how much I was longing for him. The minute we were at the house alone, we were in my bedroom, doing things that made the birds on the ledge outside blush.

"That 'weeklong' visit of Carl's turned into a three-month stay. For three months, he laid up in my daddy's house and had his way with me. He told me he loved me, and me with my country, fool-ass, I believed him. I never once even stopped to think that love's not about words. It's about actions. Love's not about taking. It's about giving. But it works both ways. It's a reciprocal thing; and when one person is doing all the giving, and the other one is doing all of the taking, that's not love. I don't know what that is, but it sure in the hell ain't love.

"I acted a fool and got pregnant. He begged me to get rid

of the child, but I said no. I wanted to go to my parents and tell them just how much I loved Carl, and that I wanted to marry him. When I told my daddy, he went to Carl and asked him if it was true. And that bastard stood there and told my daddy that every time we had been alone, I had flounced around him half-naked, trying to get him to go to bed with me. He said that he had given in once, but that it had never happened again." She sniffled and wiped the fresh tears.

"My daddy tried to beat the *black* off of me. Carl just packed his rags, got his guitar, and left. I left home a week later because I couldn't stand the way that my daddy looked at me every time I walked into the room. This look of disgust and betrayal. That look hurt me a thousand times worse than any beating could have. I went to work doing after-hours cleaning at a nightclub. The owner let me live in a little room upstairs. Your granddaddy used to hang out over there, shooting dice and taking everybody's money. He wanted me the first day he saw me, but I wasn't ready for another relationship. After what Carl and Daddy had both done to me, I never saw men in quite the same way. I promised myself that I would never love another man.

"Then, I miscarried my baby, and it seemed like nothing mattered to me anymore. The only reason that I married Pick, your grandfather, was because he had a house, a car, and some money; and I was broke and desperate. We had a house full of daughters, and I loved them with everything in me, but I kept my promise to never love another man. I spent thirty years with Pick, and I can't say that I ever once felt that I loved him. But I did feel that I needed him. He was my security."

She looked up at me for the first time since beginning her tale.

"And that's why I raised y'all like I did," she concluded. "I didn't want you to look to a man for love—only for security. I guess I thought I would save y'all some heartache like that." She sighed as she shook her head. "Seems like it all blew up in my face, though, because all I see when I look at each one of you is me at sixteen years old. All taking different paths, but all heading in the same miserable direction."

"Why are you telling me all this now, Granny?" I tried to keep the heftiness out of my own voice.

"I'm telling you this because my daughters are all too far gone now, but that doesn't mean that I can't still reach you. Maybe I was wrong for trying to make you believe that you shouldn't fall in love. That's one of the best things that can happen to a woman when it's the right kind of love.

"*This* particular love doesn't seem to love you in return, though, Kyla. Not in the way that you need. Not in the way that you deserve. All I see you doing is trying to force it. But love doesn't work like that, baby. It's not supposed to be that hard. Love just happens."

I shook my head and met her gaze. That was when I saw that look in her eyes. That same look that I had seen in Mal's eyes the morning that he had told me Shard was gone. That look of pity.

"You can't compare *my* situation to whatever happened to you in the past," I told Granny. "Shard's not that man who left you. Shard left because he wanted to make a better life for us. He *always* intended to come back for me. If he didn't care about me, then he never would have kept in touch with me. He would've just moved away and never spoken to me again." I shook my head. "You're still carrying that grudge around. Just because that man hurt you, you think that all men are like him."

"No. I'm not talking about all men, Kyla. I'm talking about Shard. And I'm not even trying to take away from his character. I'm not trying to say that he's a bad person. It's not my place to judge nobody. I see the way that you worship him, though; and I also see the way that he takes full advantage of that. You're the giver, Kyla. He's the taker. I'm telling you now, baby, if you don't realize that you're worth more than that, then nobody is ever gonna give you more."

I put my hands up to silence her. "I don't *want* more. Don't you understand that? I just want him, Granny. And whatever comes along with him, then I guess that's what I need."

"Wants and needs are two different things, Kyla."

"Not in this case," I replied softly. Then I turned and walked out of the room.

Eight

I didn't expect to receive my grandmother's blessing after the conversation we'd had. She had done something for me that she had never done before.

She had bared her soul to me.

Instead of appreciating her for what she had done, I resented her. I had not wanted to hear her tragic tale about a love gone wrong. I had not wanted an explanation as to why she had tried to raise her children the way that she had. All I wanted was for her to be happy for me. As long as *I* was happy, that was all that mattered, right? At least, that was what I was trying to tell myself as Nina and I sorted through a rack of designer jeans in Modish that Wednesday.

"I wish I could go to Miami with you," said Nina as she

removed a pair of hip-huggers that had been ripped in suggestive places and held them up for me to consider. She was the only person that I had trusted enough to tell where I was *actually* going.

"I wish you could, too," I said. Then I laughed and shook my head. "No, I don't. I haven't seen my man in five months, girl. I ain't trying to share our time together with *nobody.*"

Nina laughed, too. "Go try these on." She pushed the sexy jeans toward me. "You'll look real good in 'em." She rushed to another rack to find a top that would complement the pants. "When did Shard say that you could go and get all your clothes out of the house? You had the flyest gear around here. It would be a shame to just leave all that stuff behind."

I shrugged my shoulders. "I don't know what's up with that. I'm not worried about trying to be fly anyway. Shard is a hardworking man now. He doesn't care about trying to keep a high profile anymore, so I shouldn't either."

Nina nodded her head. "I guess not. Look on the bright side. Now that he's gone legit, he'll be able to spend a lot more quality time with you."

I smiled. "Yeah, that's the best part."

By the time we left Modish, I had almost finished off the last of the money I had been saving over the past months. My arms were loaded with bags containing jeans, three sexy, a couple of sexy tops, a slinky black spaghetti-strap dress, and a pair of stiletto sandals. I wanted Shard to see me looking just as good as I had looked before he had left. Before I had gotten pregnant. Before so many things had changed.

That night, I packed my small suitcase while Prince sat in his swing, watching me. I avoided eye contact with him, afraid that I would see something in him that would make me feel even guiltier for leaving. I was also avoiding Granny. She and I had been rather reserved with each other ever since the discussion that we'd had.

The atmosphere inside of the house felt different that evening. Strangely calm and low-keyed. Jazz stayed locked away inside her bedroom, and Granny remained on the living-room couch, chatting with one of her girlfriends over the cordless phone. I knew this because I had checked the living room several times to see if she had ended her conversation. I was anxious to call Shard and remind him of the scheduled arrival time for my flight.

When I finished packing my clothes and toiletries, I zipped both my suitcase and shoulder bag with a flourish. I turned then to look at Prince and discovered that he had fallen fast asleep. I smiled and walked over to lift him gently out of the swing. Then I planted a soft kiss on his cheek and nuzzled his neck with my nose. He smelled so good. I laid him down and wondered for the hundredth time in the past hour how I was going to leave him for three whole nights. He had been my comfort, my stability, and my peace of mind for the past four months, and I had been his. In the past couple of weeks, everyone had noticed how much he had begun to cling to me. Whenever he cried, it seemed that I was the only one who could comfort him.

"He's spoiled to you now," Granny had said.

It probably sounds strange, but I actually liked the way

that my presence alone gave him reassurance and comfort. I had never had that kind of effect on anybody. I turned on the radio and then sat on the mattress and watched Prince sleep for a few moments. After he didn't stir, I stood and headed to the living room to clean up the mess that I had made earlier.

Granny had finally vacated the couch and was closed in her bedroom. I could hear the lively voice that she reserved for gossiping over the blare of her television. I walked to the living room and parted the Venetian blinds to make sure that Will was still out in front of the house. Though the sun was dipping below the horizon, the streetlights had not come on yet. All of the kids in the neighborhood knew that a lit streetlight was the universal indicator for the outdoor curfew.

I could see Will passing a football to one of the five kids that were occupying the empty street with him. Just as I started to turn away, a set of slow-moving headlights came to a halt right by our curb. I squinted, trying to recognize the vehicle, but it was nearly impossible to see the exact color and body type from where I was positioned. Ignoring it, I closed the blinds and proceeded to pick up empty bottles, clothes, a pacifier, and a box of baby powder, but I nearly dropped all of the items when I heard a series of short, firm knocks at the front door.

"Just a minute," I called, slightly annoyed by the interruption. I figured that it was one of Jazz's latest prospects, stopping by to spend a little bit of time with her before her all-too-famous "no visitors after eleven o'clock" rule came into effect for the night. Neatly juggling everything in the crook of one arm, I used my free hand to pull the door open. Standing on the front stoop was a tall dark figure. I squinted again and leaned closer to the glass storm door.

I soon realized who it was.

"Devin?" I called.

"Hey," he said through the door, giving me a little wave.

I quickly unlatched the lock.

"Come on in." I held the door open for him. "I would hug you, but ..." I gestured toward the armload of baby paraphernalia.

"Oh, it's cool." He lingered in the doorway. "I'm sorry to just drop in on you like this. Are you real busy?"

"No. It's okay. I'll be right back." I went into the kitchen and dumped everything on the countertop. Then I leaned heavily on its surface and took a deep breath. I wasn't prepared to see anyone from as far back in my past as Devin.

Devin Halmond had been my first boyfriend, the boy I had lost my virginity to. When Devin had gone off to college to play basketball, I had begun to date Shard. Upon one of his visits home, I had dumped Devin, who had warned me that I would someday live to regret my decision. I already had to deal with every type of "I-told-you-so" and "you-should've-known-better" imaginable. I didn't feel like hearing anyone else's opinion of what was wrong with my life. I knew I had to face him, though. I couldn't run from him or anybody else. I reminded myself that my life was my business, and I had no reason to justify my choices to anyone. I turned and slowly walked back to the living room. Devin was still standing there by the door.

"How ya been?" I stopped in front of the coffee table

and folded my arms over my chest.

"Good. What about you? You been doing okay?"

"Yeah," I said without hesitation. "I've been *real* good."

I slowly sat down and waved toward the couch. "Have a seat."

He strode over and sat down next to me. His smooth black skin shined in contrast with the deep maroon T-shirt that he wore. He had grown a thin mustache since the last time that I had seen him.

"So ... I heard that you have a baby now," he said.

"Yeah. He's in there sleeping. I just laid him down a few minutes ago."

Devin grinned. "Imagine that. Kyla is a mommy now."

"I know, huh? That's got to be the craziest thing to happen since they sent men to the moon."

As our laughter died down, I waited for the question that I knew was lurking just below the surface of our small talk. The inevitable question about Shard and his whereabouts. Devin didn't delve into that topic, though. Instead, he rubbed his palms apprehensively over his long legs, brushing imaginary wrinkles out of his jeans. He gazed at me and then suddenly reached out for my hair. I reflexively moved away from his touch.

"My bad," he said, obviously embarrassed as he pulled his hand back. "I was just looking at your hair. It got a lot longer."

"Oh ... yeah." I fingered a lock of my mane, which had grown halfway down my back in the past year.

"So what you doing now?" I asked after a few tense

moments. "You still playing basketball for Marquette?"

"Nah, I just graduated in May. I lucked up and got offered a decent job in U City doing some computer work at one of the city offices down there."

"Really? That's good, Devin. I'm happy for you."

"Yeah. It ain't exactly the dream that I had to be a guard for the Nets, but hey ... it'll pay the bills. I had to find out the hard way that high-school popularity doesn't always follow you into adulthood. You have to pave your own way out here."

"So when are you moving back home?"

"It's already a done deal. I moved back last weekend. My brother had lined up an apartment and everything for me, so it's all good."

I couldn't help but feel a bit envious of the fact that Devin had already gotten his degree and was preparing to reap the rewards of his dedication to his college education. If things had gone the way that I had originally planned, I would have been entering the fall semester of my junior year at Washington.

I sighed wistfully as Devin slowly stood to his feet. "Well, listen," he said, "it's getting late, so I better head home. I was in the neighborhood, and I just stopped to see how you were and to congratulate you on having your baby." I stood, too, so that I could walk him to the door.

"Fred was telling me that he saw Nina a couple months ago," he added. "She said that you're working down at Miller Construction. You enjoying that?"

"I'm not working there anymore. I quit because I'm moving in August."

Devin turned around suddenly and looked at me as if I had just punched him in his back.

"You are? Where are you going?"

I was hesitant. I still didn't want to risk leaking out Shard's location.

"To be with my child's father."

Devin seemed to understand that I didn't want to elaborate on the details. Still, I wanted him to know that Shard and I were still a couple, in spite of anything that he might have heard to the contrary. I wanted him to know that Shard had only left me so that he could provide a better life for me.

"So ... you're still with him?"

"Yeah. We had to be apart for a while, but things are coming together now."

"Well, if you're happy, then I guess that's good news."

"I'm happy," I assured him as I opened the door for him. I followed him out to the stoop, where he turned again and reached out to gently squeeze my shoulder. I looked into his eyes and saw nothing more than genuine concern.

"You take care of yourself," he said. Before I could reply, he stepped from the stoop and started to his vehicle.

I folded my arms over my chest again and hugged myself tight. "I will," I said softly before heading back into the house.

◊ ◊ ◊ ◊

I awoke with a start the next morning and sat straight up in bed, my heart pounding, my chest heaving up and down, and my mouth as dry as the cotton in my sheets. My breath came in short gasps as my eyes darted wildly around my bedroom. It was still dark. Slowly, my eyes came into focus, and I gazed at the digital clock on my bedside table. It was four fifteen.

The sun had not even peeked over the horizon yet. I reached over to flick on the lamp and immediately looked at Prince. He was stretched out on his stomach, his chubby hands balled into tight fists. His cherubic face glowed peacefully under my lamplight. I placed my hand over his small back, rubbing it gently through his tiny blue T-shirt. I felt dazed as I slowly lay down again, trying to figure out what had jostled me awake. I couldn't recall having any nightmares. Nothing seemed out of the ordinary inside my room. There had been no logical explanation for my frantic episode.

Maybe this is a bad omen, I thought. *Maybe I shouldn't be leaving Prince here for the weekend. What if something goes wrong? What if something happens to him while I'm gone? I would never forgive myself.*

I snuggled closer to him and stroked his curls. He didn't stir. I closed my eyes and tried to find sleep again, but I couldn't. By the time seven o'clock rolled around, I had only gotten a total of twenty minutes of slumber since I had abruptly awakened. Prince was the first member of the household to awaken. As soon as I sat up on the mattress, his face took on an irritated frown and his lips turned down into a pout. Seconds later, his cries rang out over the still morning air.

"Okay," I crooned softly as I picked him up and held him against my shoulder. "Okay, I got you." I patted his back while I stood up with him and headed to the kitchen to heat one of his prepared bottles. I was setting the bottle in a saucepan of hot water when Jazz came walking into the room, her face set in mid-yawn.

"Oh, what's the matter?" she asked Prince in an exaggerated mock baby voice. "What's the matter, man?" She peered at him over my shoulder. "You hungry? Your momma moving too slow with your breakfast?"

She suddenly looked at me and frowned. "Kyla, don't you have to be at the airport soon? What time is your flight?"

"Five after nine. Nina is picking me up in an hour."

"Here," Jazz reached for Prince, "give me the baby so you can go and get ready. You're gonna be late."

"I got him. He probably won't take it from you anyway. He likes it when I feed him."

"Kyla, it's food, girl. If he's hungry, he doesn't care *who's* giving it to him. He wouldn't care if Freddy Krueger was holding that bottle. Now give him to me."

I sighed and reluctantly passed Prince to her. For some reason, I just didn't want to let him go that morning. The only thing that pushed me into the shower was the thought of flying to Florida. I was anticipating seeing Shard just as much as I was dreading leaving Prince. But my heart started to thump with excitement as I pushed the shower curtain back and wrapped my svelte body in a fluffy pink towel. After patting my skin dry, I moisturized it with a sweet-smelling Chanel lotion and misted it with Chanel body splash. The low-cut jeans that I had purchased at Modish rode my ample hips and displayed a small fragment of my lean, flat stomach. The faux diamond chandelier earrings I wore set the half-casual, half-elegant ensemble off.

I turned my back to the mirror and then peeled the waist of my jeans down half an inch so that I could see my entire tattoo that proclaimed, "Shard's baby girl" which was scrawled on my back. Then I smiled as I ran my fingertip over the permanent declaration, realizing that I could now barely contain myself. I rushed around the house, searching for my clear, strappy, stiletto sandals.

By the time Nina walked into the living room, I had my purse and duffel bag over one shoulder and a small bag for my toiletries and shoes over the other. Jazz sat on the couch, feeding Prince and staring at the television, while Will lounged on the recliner, eating a bowl of cereal. As soon as Nina saw the baby, she rushed to the couch and leaned over Jazz.

"Hey, Prince," Nina cooed, planting kisses all over his face. "Hey, cutie. Gimme some of that bottle. Gimme some, Prince."

I bit my lip as I watched her playing with him. I suddenly felt that feeling coming over me again. That same feeling that had gripped me earlier that morning. Except this time, I understood its origins. I realized what it was that I really felt. I felt torn.

My heart felt like it was being tugged in two different directions. Being sliced and divided between two people, both of equal importance in my life. One of them was right here in St. Louis. The other was in Miami. In order to be with one, I had to temporarily leave the other. My eyes filled with warm water, and I blinked rapidly, trying to prevent the tears from spilling.

"Move, Nina." I walked over to the couch. "Let me say

bye to him." She stepped aside so that I could bend and plant a kiss on Prince's forehead, and then on each of his cheeks. I gripped my shoulder bag tightly as a tear escaped my eye and splattered onto his soft skin. When I stood upright, all eyes were on me.

"You crying, Kyla?" asked Jazz with a concerned frown.

"No." I quickly dashed the tears from my face. I sniffled and turned my back before I could completely melt down in front of everyone. "Let's go, Nina. Bye, everybody."

"Bye," I heard Will and Jazz chorus.

"I'm surprised Granny isn't up yet," said Nina as we walked out to the curb together.

"Granny probably doesn't want to say bye. She's been against me going on this trip ever since I told her about it."

Nina unlocked the car doors, and I dropped my bags in the backseat before I climbed up front. "Why you think she's against it?"

I gave her a long, steady gaze. "You know why, Nina. You know why she doesn't like Shard. You know why none of them like him, including your momma."

Nina frowned. "Because he slangs?"

"No. That's not the real reason. He's not slanging anymore anyway, so they can't judge him for mistakes that he's made in the past."

"What makes you think that they don't like him then?"

I stared hard at her, my eyebrow raised in a "don't-play-me-for-a-sucker" look.

"*What?*"

"Because of what happened that time ... between him and Jazz."

Nina bit her lip and squirmed uncomfortably. "Oh ... *that.*"

"See? I *knew* that you knew about it." I gazed at the road ahead of me. "I knew that somebody had told you. They all blame Shard for that, but he didn't initiate it. You know Jazz just as well as I do. Everybody knows how she flirts with niggas and tries to play her mind games to get what she wants."

"I don't think Jazz would go after your boyfriend on purpose, though. I don't think that she would try to hurt *anybody* in the family like that on purpose."

"Mmph." I rolled my eyes and shook my head. "I see they got to you, too. Got you thinking that they're all perfect and that they have such high moral standards. You know, Granny tried to tell me the other night that she raised them that way because she didn't want them to get hurt by men."

"Raised them *what* way?"

I narrowed my eyes at her. "Please don't sit there and act like you don't know what I'm talking about. You know how they are. The badass, gold-digging, man-stealing Brown women." I sneered. "You must be so proud to come from a family of such upstanding ladies," I added sarcastically.

"Why are you talking about them like that? We're all family, Kyla. No matter what we do, we'll always be family. That used to be important to you."

"I know that." I dug in my purse for my tube of Champagne lip gloss. "And family is still very important to me.

But I have my own family now. Just because Granny screwed hers up, that doesn't mean that she can try to screw mine up by telling me that Shard ain't right for me. Who is she to give advice?"

Nina was silent.

"You don't have to answer that," I said icily as I spread the gloss over my lips. "I don't care what any of y'all think about me. After August, y'all won't have to deal with me anymore anyway."

"Ugh, what is up with you? You hadn't complained about any of this since you moved back home. But now that you're about to see Shard, your whole demeanor has changed. All of a sudden, you got attitude and negativity towards everybody. You're acting the way you used to act when he was here." She looked at me and added, "That's why I don't think that Granny and them dislike him because of what happened with Jazz. I think they dislike him because ..."

"Because of what?"

She hesitated before replying, "Because of the way that *you* are when you're with him. You didn't come home for almost two years. Everybody thought that he had talked you against the family. They all thought that he was keeping you away. And then, when he left you—"

"Left me? He never *left* me, Nina. You know why he had to get out of St. Louis. And he never kept me away from anybody. I kept myself away." We were both silent for a moment. "So how come you never said any of this before?" I finally asked. "If you thought that he was 'controlling my mind,' then why didn't you ever say anything about it to me?"

"I didn't say I thought that he was controlling your mind. I'm just telling you what the rest of the family was thinking. *I'm* not trying to tell you how you should live your life. I never have. If you know deep down in your heart that Shard is good for you, then it ain't nobody's business but yours. I wish you the best."

"It's nice to finally hear somebody say that."

When Nina pulled into the parking lot at Lambert Airport, I was pushing the door open before she could even depress the brake pedal.

"Dang. Can we at least come to a complete stop first?" she asked with a laugh. I laughed too, but I was already leaning over the seat to grab the handle of one of my bags. Nina climbed out of the car and opened the back passenger door so that she could get the other bag for me. "It's already warm here, so you know it's probably going to be *scorching* in Miami. Did you pack some cool clothes?"

"Yep." I ignored the stares from two guys who were exiting the airport as we were entering. "What time is it?"

She flipped open her cell phone and gazed at the display. "It's eight-twenty."

I stopped in my tracks and reached out for the bag she had been carrying. "I can take it from here."

"You sure you don't need any help?"

"I'm sure."

"All right then," she said with a soft sigh as she passed me the bag and then leaned forward to give me a quick hug. "Have a safe trip." I nodded and leaned into her hug, even though my arms were too full to return it. "And I'll tell Granny that you said bye."

I rolled my eyes. "You don't have to tell her *nothing*. But you can give Prince another kiss for me when you see him. Will you do that?"

"You know I will. Don't forget to call me when you make it."

"I won't forget."

I watched Nina wave, and then turn and head in the opposite direction. As I made my way across the freshly buffed airport floor, I felt the eyes of several passersby following me. I felt like I had back in high school when I had stopped all those hearts and conversations.

My excitement had risen to dizzying heights. By the time I had checked my bags and sat next to the window on the plane, my entire body was quaking. I popped a piece of bubble gum into my mouth and chomped violently on it as I watched other passengers board the plane. Suddenly, a petite, elderly white woman with blue-rinsed hair turned and edged over to the vacant seat right next to mine. She smiled widely, showing pearl-white dentures as she slowly lowered her body to a sitting position.

"Good morning," she greeted me with a nod.

"Hi," I replied.

An elderly man, whom I assumed was her husband, sat on the seat at the end of the row, right next to her. He looked past her and at me. He, too, smiled and nodded.

"How are you?" he greeted me.

"Fine," I said politely. I began to anticipate a very dull flight. I lay my head back on my seat and closed my eyes, drifting away into my own little space.

"Would you like a stick of gum?" I heard the woman's voice offer.

I opened my eyes and smiled at her. "No. I have some, thank you." She nodded, but continued to gaze at me as she dropped the package of Juicy Fruit back into her bag. When my eyes met hers, she smiled even brighter and wider.

"I hope you will forgive me for staring," she said. "But I think that you are just *darling*." She looked at the man next to her. "Isn't she, Jim? Isn't she darling?"

"Yes," the man agreed as he looked at me and nodded his head. "She's very lovely."

"Thank you," I said to the both of them.

"My name is Katherine Watson," said the woman as she presented a small, wrinkled hand. "And this is my husband, Jim." I took her hand in mine and shook it; and then I reached across her to shake Jim's hand.

"I'm Kyla."

"Nice to meet you," they chorused.

"Are you from St. Louis?" asked Katherine.

"Yes."

"Jim and I are from Atlanta," replied Katherine. "We have a lot of family here in St. Louis, though. Our oldest son, Ted, lives here. He was in an automobile accident last Sunday. We've been here with him since Sunday night."

"Oh," I said as my voice filled with sympathy. "I hope

he's okay now."

"He's in stable condition," piped Jim as he leaned forward to look at me. "He had some broken bones and a concussion, but he'll recover quickly. He's a real trooper."

I gave him a sincere smile. "I'm sure he is."

By the time the aircraft was cruising at its highest altitude, I had learned a lot about Jim and Katherine. I learned that they had been married for fifty-one years. I also learned that they had four children and nine grandchildren.

"Would you like to know the key to a long, happy marriage?" asked Katherine after she told me how many years they had been together.

"What?" I asked.

"No TV in the bedroom," she replied saucily. I cracked up laughing while Jim turned as red as a cherry tomato. "No," said Katherine after our laughter subsided, "but the real key is understanding. You'll often hear people say that trust and communication are the most important factors; but *we* strongly believe that it's a simple matter of understanding. How can you communicate with or trust someone that you can't even understand? Even though we don't always agree with one another, we *always* try to understand each other. Isn't that right, Jim?"

I watched with a smile as he nodded and lovingly patted her knee. I was astonished when the captain came over the intercom to announce that we were preparing to land in Atlanta. Katherine gazed down at her delicate gold wristwatch.

"Oh my." She placed a hand over her heart. "It's already eleven thirty-five. I can't believe that we talked the entire flight!"

"I know," I agreed. I was pleasantly surprised by how much I had enjoyed their company. I almost hated to say good-bye to them when we were finally given the green light to unbuckle our seat belts and deplane.

"Have fun in Miami," Jim told me as we separated inside the terminal.

I thanked them and waved as they walked away.

In Atlanta, I had to wait until 1:15 for the flight that would take me to Miami. On that flight, I was seated next to a thirty-something professional-looking black woman. She was dressed in a dark blue skirt and jacket, and her hair was pulled back in a neat bun. She offered me a small smile, and I returned it, but she and I were silent for the first thirty minutes or so of the flight. I flipped through the *Essence* magazine that I had pur-chased at the airport, but I found that it was extremely difficult to focus on the contents of the pages.

I began to worry about Prince. I wondered if he was missing me. Was he crying for me at that very moment? My eyes almost filled with tears again, until I suddenly thought about Shard. Then I smiled. I was actually going to see him in less than three hours. It seemed so unreal. I didn't have the slightest idea of what to expect when I saw him. Would he look hopeless and down-trodden? Tired and worn-out? Or just plain unfulfilled and unsatisfied? I had never seen him with those emotions on his face. He had always been confident and extremely focused. What if the cruel perils of life had stripped him of those quali-ties over the past five months?

I was pulled out of my musings by the voice of the woman sitting next to me.

"Excuse me," she leaned over and whispered. "Are you still reading your magazine?"

I looked down and realized that the closed periodical was teetering over my knee. "Oh, no." I passed it to her. "You can read it."

We both grew silent as she flipped it open and began to leaf through the pages. I took my mental leave of the woman and gazed out the small window. Every time I flew, I was amazed by the sight of the wispy white clouds that hovered nearby. How could something that appeared so thick and lush from the earth be so flimsy and insubstantial up close?

It was ironic how things could appear one way when viewed from a certain angle, but turn out to be something so completely different from another angle. I lay my head back on the headrest and just stared out the window until the announcement for landing rang out over the intercom. Then I immediately sat up straighter in my seat.

The woman next to me looked at me and grinned. "Are you excited?" She passed me the *Essence* as we landed. "Ooh, girl, look at you. You are trembling."

I bit my lip as I clutched the magazine to my chest. The woman and I unbuckled our seat belts and stood up almost simultaneously at first sight of the indicator light. Then I took a deep breath and followed the line of passengers down through the terminal and into Miami International Airport.

Nine

As soon as I was inside the main airport building, I was craning my neck, looking all around me for Shard. The building was huge, and it practically hummed with the sounds of people hustling and bustling to various destinations. I stepped out of the way of the other passengers as I stuck my thumbnail between my teeth and scanned the crowds. Then I frowned, wondering if I had given Shard the correct time of my scheduled arrival.

"Shit." I dug in my bag for some change so that I could use a payphone.

"Looking for somebody?" a familiar voice suddenly boomed behind me. I whirled around and gasped.

"Mal!" I shrieked.

"What's up, baby girl?" Mal smiled brightly as he

walked over to me. I flung my arms around his neck. "You know you look unbelievable," he declared as he kissed my cheek. He then grasped both my hands in his and gently pushed me back so that he could get a better look at me.

"There ain't no way that you had a baby, Kyla." I twirled around for him, making a complete 360-degree turn. "That body is even hotter than it was when I first met you." He shook his head and whistled. "*Damn*."

We headed toward baggage claim together. Mal looked great. He wore a cool-looking pale yellow cotton shirt and a pair of brown, loose-fitting shorts that hung nearly to his ankles. He looked as if he had gained a few pounds, but he wore them very well.

I grinned as I stood on tiptoes to pat his low-cut hair. "You cut the hair off, Mal?" I could hardly believe that the three inches of hair he had always worn had been peeled to borderline bald.

"Yes ma'am. This heat down here is no joke. I couldn't handle all the extra stuff on my head."

I stared out the huge airport windows as we walked. "Ooh, I can tell it's hot out there."

"Definitely," said Mal. "You gotta love it, though. Me and Shard like it a lot down here. It's carefree. It's like paradise for real."

"So ... Shard is happy? He hasn't let all this drama stress him out too much, has he?"

"Nah." Mal vigorously shook his head. "He's maintaining, so don't even stress yourself out about that."

As soon as we had rounded up all of my bags, Mal and I stepped out into the warm Miami sunshine. The air was balmy, and an occasional breeze drifted in from the Florida Keys and caressed my face as we trekked across the parking lot.

"Shard had a few errands to run," explained Mal. "That was why he sent me to pick you up." He suddenly stopped at a silver Cadillac and popped the locks. "Here. Let me drop those bags in the back for you." He placed my bags on the seat, closed the door again, and then opened the front passenger door for me.

I raised an arched eyebrow and stared at him.

"What?" he asked innocently.

"Where did the ride come from, Mal?"

"Oh, this? This is just a hookup thing that I got through my cousin, Rob. You remember hearing his name, don't you? He was the one who put us down with the situation at the dock and the apartment when we first got here. Rob has his own business. He's a successful dude, and he really wanted to help out when he found out what was going on. It's all on the up-and-up, though."

I slowly nodded and climbed into the car. Mal closed the door behind me and jogged around to the driver's side. As soon as he had climbed behind the wheel, I turned the knob and cranked the air conditioner up to the maximum level. Mal unclipped his cell from his belt and dialed a number as he shifted into gear and carefully wheeled out of the crowded lot. He pressed the speaker to his ear and waited while the call was processed.

"Ay, man," he suddenly said into the mouthpiece. "I just picked up something from the airport for you." I smiled as I realized that he was talking to Shard.

"Yeah. Something tall, light, and beautiful." He chuckled. "Yeah, man, I got her ... The flight was right on time ... Yeah. She does." Mal looked over at me, and then refocused on his conversation. "Ay, man, I'm hungry. You hungry, baby girl?" I realized that I was famished.

"Yeah," I said, nodding my head.

"How about some seafood?"

I nodded again.

"Ay, Shard, let's meet at Baleen," Mal suggested. "Ah-ight. Well, we should be there in about twenty minutes. How far are you from Coconut Grove? Ah-ight. Well, we'll see you in a little bit." He flipped the phone closed and clipped it to his belt again.

I immediately pulled down the visor overhead and inspected my face in the mirror, then brushed Great Lash mascara onto my eyelashes and reapplied the Champagne gloss to my lips until they wore a soft, dewy glow. After that, I smoothed my palms over my hair. I could feel all of the excitement of the past few days reaching an apex. It had all come down to this. As I dropped the cosmetics back into my bag, I spotted my brown leather wallet nestled inside.

"You want to see a picture of my little boy?" I asked Mal.

"Oh man, of course I do."

I removed the wallet and opened it to the thin plastic holders that contained the photos. "That was him at three months old." I passed him the open wallet. "He's a little bit bigger than that now, though."

"Damn. This kid looks *just* like Shard. This is crazy. They're almost identical."

"I know."

"That's gonna be my partna right there," said Mal excitedly. "I'm gonna have to spoil his little butt. That way, he'll always think that I'm cooler than his momma and daddy."

I chuckled and shook my head.

"Let me hang on to the picture for a little while," Mal added as an afterthought. He grinned mischievously. "I wanna use it to have a little fun with Shard when we get to the restaurant." He jimmied the photo out of its holder and passed the wallet back to me, then he slipped it into his back pocket. I gazed in quiet astonishment at the beauty of Miami as we sped along the highway. The cornflower sky seemed three times bluer here. The luxuriant grass was rich, emerald green. And the palm trees. I had never seen palm trees anywhere other than television, yet here they were, as abundant as ever along the sides of the roads standing majestically waving their fronds.

Mal drove to a nice area of the city called Coconut Grove. It was clean and very well-kept. I guessed that it was probably a hot spot for tourists. Once there, we pulled in at Baleen for a seafood dinner. It was a pretty restaurant, with a breezy, tropical atmosphere. The young, tanned hostess gave us a stark-white, sparkly Pepsodent smile, and then ushered us to a table for three. Only seconds later, another tanned young woman came bouncing over to us. She had big green eyes and her dark hair was pulled back in a tousled ponytail.

"Hello," she chirped enthusiastically. "My name is Amber, and I'll be your server this evening." She removed the leather-bound notepad from the pocket of her apron and flipped it open after passing us each a menu and leaving one at the vacant seat.

"May I take your drink orders?" she asked.

"I'll just have a glass of water with lemon, please," I said.

"Add two glasses of Patron to that, Ma," ordered Mal.

Amber nodded. "Are you guys ready to order your meal, or do you need a few more minutes to decide?"

"Let us have a few more minutes," said Mal. "We'll let you know when we're ready."

"Take your time," Amber replied. "I'll be right back with those drinks."

I opened my menu as she strolled away and scanned the list of entrees that the restaurant offered. My mouth watered as I read the descriptions underneath the selections.

"Whoa, Mal ... this stuff is kind of expensive."

"It's not too bad. Me and Shard eat here all the time. You know we ain't able to hit up the hot spots in 'The Lou' no more, so we have to improvise."

I looked around the restaurant. "Well, this isn't a bad consolation prize."

"You should try the seafood fettuccine," Mal suggested. "It's got big shrimp and crawfish in it. They give you a nice-sized serving, too."

"Sounds good to me." I closed my menu and tossed it

down on the surface of the table, then glanced around the restaurant expectantly, drumming my fingernails on the arms of the comfortable chair. Mal had assured me that Shard had been doing well, but I was still apprehensive about seeing him. He had often sounded agitated and pressured over the phone. I needed to see him for myself before I could decide whether he was indeed "maintaining," as Mal had claimed. I played with my napkin while Mal sipped on his drink.

After a few moments, I sighed and pushed my chair back from the table. "I'm going to the ladies' room." I had my hands wrapped tightly around the chair arms, preparing to push myself to a standing position, when Mal glanced over my shoulder and smiled softly.

"I don't think you want to do that right now," he said. "Take a look behind you."

My heart immediately began to thud. I slowly swiveled my head and gazed over my left shoulder. That was when I saw him.

Rashard Phaylon was sauntering through the front door, looking like a three-dimensional image of masculine perfection.

His golden skin tone had also been deepened by the sun, giving it a coppery hue. His lustrous, low-cut black hair was rippled with those deep, rich waves. On his face, he wore silvery, aviator-style sunglasses, but his thick, perfectly shaped sable eyebrows crowned the tops of the lenses. He was dressed in a sky blue, short-sleeved, button-down shirt. It had been left completely unbuttoned, and underneath, he wore a thin white cotton tank that hugged his rippled stomach and trim waist like a manufacturer's dream. He wore baggy blue jeans that sagged slightly, even though they were belted at the waist. His platinum watch caught the light that poured in through the windows as he stopped at the hostess stand and spoke briefly with her. The hostess smiled and nodded, then turned and pointed toward our table. Shard thanked her, and then began to navigate through the labyrinth that was the dining area. I saw a slow smile tugging at the corners of his mouth as he neared me. Then I realized that I was still hovering in midair over my chair, gripping the arms.

I was almost in a state of shock.

Oh, my Lord, I thought. *Miami has done the impossible. It actually made Shard even more gorgeous than he already is.*

I managed to stand erect as he stood before me. We remained there a moment, completely silent as we drank in the sight of one another. All of a sudden, I had a flashback to the night that I had met him. He bit down on his bottom lip, and even though I couldn't see his eyes, I could feel them slinking down my body. I couldn't hold back any longer. I flung my arms around his neck and held on to him, immediately feeling whole again. Tears escaped from my eyes as he embraced me.

"Let me kiss you," he said softly.

I obliged and tilted my head so that his mouth could meet mine. I got lost in that kiss, almost forgetting that we were in the middle of a restaurant. When we finally pulled apart, I was breathless.

"Aww," murmured Mal with a teasing grin. "Y'all are gonna make me cry." I laughed at him as he wiped imaginary tears from his eyes.

"Look at *you*," Shard said to me as he wrapped his fingers around my waist and gave me a little spin. "*Damn*, girl."

"She's lookin' hot, ain't she?" asked Mal, taking another sip of his drink.

"Yes, she is," agreed Shard, shaking his head as he continued to stare me down. "She's lookin' hotter than ever before." I grinned, then sat down in my chair again and crossed my legs while Shard sat in the seat adjacent to mine. I watched as he removed his sunglasses and placed them on the tabletop. All of a sudden, I was staring into those haunting, olive-black eyes. I was relieved because in them, I saw no destitution, desolation, or desperation. All I saw was the same confidence, authority, and self-assuredness that I had always seen there. Shard looked healthy and well-rested. I couldn't believe that I was sitting there next to him again after almost six whole months. It seemed too good to be true.

"How was your flight, baby girl?" asked Shard as he draped his arm over the back of my chair and opened his menu.

I gazed dreamily at him. "It was nice."

Mal suddenly stood and reached into his back pocket. "I got something to show you, man," he told Shard. I watched him produce the small photo that I had given him in the car. He slid it across the table in Shard's direction. Shard took a sip of his Patron, and then reached out to pick up the picture.

"Guess who that is," said Mal with a lopsided grin.

Shard frowned curiously as he gazed at the picture. All at once, though, his face took on a look of recognition.

"Hold up," he said with a grin as he sat up straighter in

his chair. "Is this my lil' man right here?"

Mal nodded and chuckled. "That's him. He could be your lil' *twin*, couldn't he?"

"Hell, yeah," agreed Shard as he stared at the picture of Prince in amazement. "Ay, he looks like my pops, too, right?"

"Yep," said Mal. "He definitely look like y'all. No doubt about that."

Shard seemed reluctant to lay the photo down. He just couldn't take his eyes off of his son. "Lil' dude is handsome, ain't he?" he asked with a proud grin.

"That he is," Mal agreed. "I told Kyla that he's going to be getting spoiled when he gets down here. I'm gonna take him *everywhere*. Y'all won't even have to worry about a babysitter when you need a break."

"That's nice of you, Mal," I said as I sucked the juice from my lemon wedge, "but you don't have enough experience to be alone with my baby. If he started crying too hard, you would probably start trying to read Chairman Mao to him to calm him down."

Shard cracked up laughing while Mal dropped his head and chuckled as well.

"Ah-ight. That's how you gonna play me, Kyla?"

Shard was still laughing. "She got you, man."

"Ay, don't trip on me just because I believe in the advancement of my people," said Mal. "You're damn right I'm gonna read that boy Chairman Mao. Not only that, but I'm also gonna teach him the doctrines of the Honorable Elijah Muhammad. I'm gonna read him some W.E.B. DuBois, and some Cornel West, too. I'm gonna expose him to every aspect of the experience. I'm gonna help y'all raise the next prominent black leader, ya feel me?"

"Is that right?" asked Shard with a raised eyebrow. He looked at me with a teasing smile. "Is that what you want your baby to become, Kyla? A national leader?"

I grinned as I began to play along with his game. "I don't think so," I said. "I'd rather have a linebacker for the Green Bay Packers."

"Yeah," agreed Shard. "And I think that I'd rather have a singer or a rapper. Hell, we could have four more and make it a group act."

"What?" hissed Mal.

Shard winked at me. We both knew how to push Mal's buttons. In a matter of seconds, he was going to climb up on his soapbox and chastise us for our ideals.

"See that's what's wrong with America today." Mal pointed an accusing finger at the two of us. "That's all black folks think that their kids are capable of doing. Entertaining. Why don't we ever try to encourage our kids to make strides in the sciences, mathematics, literature, and politics? We find one or two things that we like, and we limit ourselves to that.

"Everybody is trying to turn little Johnny into an athlete or a rap star. Maybe what little Johnny *really* wants to do is become a scientist so that he can discover the cure for cancer. Maybe little Johnny wants to travel to foreign nations as an ambassador so that he can bring peace to the United States and its adversaries. Or better yet, maybe Johnny wants to remain right here and fight the adversities that plague his own people in the land of his birth." He gazed at each of us. "Y'all ever thought about *that*?" he asked.

Shard shook his head. "When it comes right down to it," he told Mal, "little Johnny is going to want to do what we all have been trying to do since Lincoln freed the slaves. Make money. A man don't care if he's holding a mic or pedaling a bike. It's all about the hustle, man. As long as he sees some real dividends, he won't complain."

My smile faded as I listened to Shard's words. I had only been teasing Mal by pretending that I didn't want Prince to seek out and obtain some noble profession. I had actually agreed with Mal. I saw nothing wrong with black men pursuing lucrative careers in sports and entertainment; but I also believed that it was important for black people to realize that they were capable of achieving *all* types of success, just as Mal had stated. Shard, however, was quickly showing me that his only aspiration for Prince was that he make money. It didn't matter where or how he got it, just as long as he managed to get it.

"Wait a minute." I looked at Shard. "Are you seriously trying to say that you wouldn't care what choices your son made in his life just as long as he got paid for them?"

"No. That's not what I'm saying. What I *am* saying, though, is that most people make career choices based on how it's going to profit *them*, not how it's going to affect the rest of the world. That's the mind-set that most of these kids are growing up with."

"And I can agree with you on that," piped Mal. "That is

how a lot of people think."

"But that still doesn't make it right," I said, as I realized that Mal was now taking Shard's side. "As Prince's parents, Shard, it's our job to be sure that he's raised with the mind-set that money is *not* everything."

Shard eyed Mal, and I saw them exchange glances. They were both silent. Nobody voiced their agreement. I realized that they were suddenly sharing the same point of view. I was now their opponent in the debate.

"So y'all don't feel me on this?" I looked from one man to the other.

"It's like this, Ma," said Mal, clearing his throat. "It would be kind of naive to try to tell the kid that money ain't important. Money does make the world go 'round. It would be nice if it *didn't* matter, but it does. You could stand up right now and ask anybody in this room if it matters and see how many would give you a 'hell, yes' on that."

"So what happened to all that you were just talking about raising the next black leader, and the ambassador, and all that?" I asked Mal as I folded my arms over my chest. "You don't stand behind what you say anymore, Mal? Has leaving St. Louis changed you *that* much?"

"Come on, Kyla." Mal put his hands up defensively. "Don't start getting catty with me. This is Mal you're talking to. You know I always stand behind what I say. I did say that black folk needed to teach their kids that there are other ways to be a success in life other than the ways that everybody's after. But the key word here is *success*. I said it's okay to be a scientist or a politician. I never once said that it was okay to be broke."

Shard nodded in agreement.

"What's my last name, Shard?" asked Mal.

"*Rich*-mond," sang out Shard in a fake, exaggerated Jamaican accent.

"And what do I have to do?" asked Mal with a grin.

"Ya got-ta stay *rich,* mon," cracked Shard. They reached across the table to slap a solidarity shake. I shook my head and rolled my eyes.

"I can't believe y'all don't feel me," I mumbled with disappointment as I reopened my menu, resigning myself to the relinquishment of the argument.

"Don't even trip, baby," said Shard softly as he rubbed his hand over my back. "As soon as we finish here, I'm gonna take you home and feel you as long as you want me to."

Mal grinned and nodded. "Spoken like a true player," he praised.

The debate became a forgotten issue as I tried to pretend that Shard's words and his touch were not fazing me; but in actuality, I was burning with desire for him. It had been five very long months since we had been together. Five months, three weeks, three days, and six hours to be exact. I didn't want to wait another minute for him. After we had eaten, the three of us walked out of the restaurant together.

"I'll get your bags," Shard said as he handed me his keys. "Go 'head and turn the air on in the car. It's the black sedan on the row towards the middle of the lot." I nodded as I accepted the keys. Then I leaned over for Mal to give me a quick kiss on the cheek.

"I'll see you later, baby girl," he said with a smile.

"Bye," I called. I walked carefully across the lot in my stilettos, searching for the black sedan near the middle row. I only saw three black cars spread out over the area. One was a four-door early model Corolla. I aimed the keyless entry remote at the vehicle and pressed the button that should have unlocked the doors. The vehicle did not respond.

I strolled a little farther down the row and stopped at the late model black Malibu. This car did not respond either. I frowned, turned slowly, and gazed down the row at the only other black sedan near the center of the lot.

An X-Type Jaguar.

I told myself that there was no way that *this* was the car that Shard was driving. Still, I aimed the remote at the luxurious vehicle and pressed the unlock button. The shrill, unmistakable sound of an alarm disarming rang out over the air. The headlights flashed, and the door locks popped. I headed slowly over to the car, grasped the silver handle of the front passenger door, and pulled. Smooth gray leather, rich, dark wood-grain, and sleek chrome welcomed me to the interior of the plush automobile. I slid into the passenger seat, and the coveted "new car smell" wafted up to my nostrils. Once I located the key and stuck it into the ignition, then turned it on, the car came to life and purred so softly it was nearly impossible to tell whether it was even running. I cranked up the air conditioner and just sat there in shocked silence.

I was still admiring the car when Shard pulled the back

door open and dropped my bags inside. I stared at him when he climbed into the driver's seat.

"You and Mal sure are rolling hard," I declared. "I never seen two people who work on a dock pull in enough bank to roll around in Cadillacs and Jags."

He was silent as he pushed on the CD player, making the speakers pound like steel drums with the bass from a rap song. I automatically reached out to turn down the volume.

"Hello?" I waved a hand in front of his eyes to get his attention. "Are you even listening to me?"

He shifted into gear. "I hear you."

"So ... aren't you gonna answer me?"

"You didn't ask me anything." He turned the volume up to ear-splitting level again. Again, I turned it down.

"What you doing? Stop tripping with the radio."

"What's the deal then?" I demanded as I studied his handsome profile. "How did you get this car? You ain't making Jaguar-money now. Is that where all the money was going that you had me sending to you? You were using that to make payments on this car?"

"How you gonna question me about what I been doing with my own money? If I *was* using it for that, so what?"

"But you told me you were saving that money. You said that it was for when me and Prince got down here in August. Don't tell me that you spent it all on this car."

Shard chuckled. "Now this is comical. I know *you* ain't over here getting steamed about money. After you just gave that Nobel Prize speech about how unimportant it is?"

"That was different. And you know that it was. Right now, I'm talking about our *life*. What are we going to have to fall back on if that money is all gone?"

"The money ain't gone nowhere, Kyla," said Shard as he wheeled into the flow of traffic. "It's still there, ah-ight?"

I sighed with relief, but then frowned as I realized that I was now even more confused than I had been before. "Then how'd you get the car?"

"I got a deal on it. Mal's cousin, Rob, knows some people in high places at a dealership. You know how we do. He hooked us up."

"That's *some* hookup. This car is brand-new, isn't it?"

"It's a few months old."

I settled back in my seat and grew silent. He looked over at me after a moment and murmured, "So I guess if you're flipping out about the ride, then I probably should go ahead and prepare you for the spot that I'm staying in."

"I ain't tripping about your apartment. You already told me that it was small—"

"Nah. Listen," Shard interrupted, "I don't live in the apartment anymore. I was just there for a month. I live on this side of town now. Here in Coconut Grove."

"You do?"

"Yeah. I live in a condo about fifteen minutes away."

"A condo? How did you—"

"Just hear me out," said Shard as he interrupted me again. "It's much cleaner and safer in this area than it was at the other spot that I had."

"Yeah, but—"

"Just listen. I don't want to go into details about everything right now. I just want you to understand that I'm trying to look out for you and Prince. All this is for y'all."

"Is it all still legit, though?" I asked.

"Kyla, haven't I done this thing the way that I told you that I was going to do it from the jump? Didn't I tell you that I was going to keep you out of the line of fire when the heat came down? Didn't I tell you that I was going to get you down here with me as soon as I could?"

"Yeah."

"And haven't I done all that?"

"Yeah."

"Well, then, cut me some slack," he said. "No secrets, no lies. I need you to just trust me. You ain't here to worry and fret about anything anyway. You're here to relax and enjoy this weekend. Can you just do that for me?"

As I looked into those eyes of his, I knew that resistance was futile.

"Yeah, I guess I can do that."

Ten

Shard's condominium was an ultramodern white dwelling with glossy hardwood floors, textured walls, and floor-to-ceiling windows that looked out over the city and the sparkling Atlantic Ocean in the distance.

It was absolutely breathtaking.

All of the furniture in the two-bedroom condo was black leather and chrome. The chairs and sofa in the living room were complemented well by the chrome and glass coffee table that served as the centerpiece. A 32-inch plasma television hung on the wall over the fireplace. Even the master bedroom was decorated solely in black, gray, and chrome.

I felt strangely unsettled by the luxurious beauty of Shard's home. What had become of the cramped, one-bedroom apartment in the slums that he had often complained to me about? What had become of the struggles and the hardships that he had allegedly faced on a daily basis? Nothing added up. I didn't ask any more questions, though. I wanted to show him that I did indeed trust him. As I was standing in the kitchen, staring at the Olympic-sized swimming pool out of the circular window, I felt Shard ease up behind me and wrap his arms around my waist.

"I'm glad you're here."

"So am I."

He gathered my hair in his hand and moved it away from my neck so that he could plant soft, moist kisses on my skin. I closed my eyes and bit my lip, feeling my whole body ignite with passion. He pulled me back firmly against his chest and thighs, allowing me to feel his desire through the material of his jeans.

"Wait," I whispered hoarsely as his hands went for the closure on my pants.

"Come on. It's been damn near six months. How much longer do you want me to wait?"

"I just remembered something," I breathed as his hands vacated my jeans and went underneath my top.

"What you remember? You remember how much fun we used to have when we got down? You remember how good it felt?"

"Yeah," I moaned, feeling my eyes roll back in my head as he introduced the memory. I quickly regained my composure, though, and managed to pull away from him. "Nah, I just remembered something else. I need to check on Prince."

He passed his phone to me. "Do what you gotta do."

I blocked Shard's number and dialed Granny's house phone while he wrapped me in his embrace again and rested his chin on my shoulder. I pressed the phone speaker against my ear. As the extension rang, Shard began to kiss my neck again.

"Hello?" answered Nina.

"Hey, girl."

"What's happenin', chick? You in the MIA yet?"

"Yep. I been here for a couple of hours, actually. I forgot to call."

"How can you forget something like that?" she scolded. "Granny's been sitting up here about to freak out, worrying about you."

"Really?" *Serves her right,* I thought. *While she was trying to be stubborn this morning, she should have been coming out to say bye to me.* A moan escaped my throat as Shard began nuzzling the base of my neck with his mouth.

"You still here?" asked Nina.

"Uh, yeah. Where's my baby?"

"In my lap right now. Drifting off to sleep."

"What? Girl, it's not even 5 o'clock yet. Don't put him to sleep. You're gonna get him all off balance. He'll be up half the night."

"So? That's gonna be Granny's problem. She can handle it."

"You are so hardheaded," I fussed. "I'm not concerned about Granny right now. I'm trying to tell you that I don't want my baby awake all night, Nina. He's gonna be fussy and cranky.

And then he'll cry himself sick."

"He's going to do that anyway. If I try to keep him from sleeping, he'll start screaming."

"Just forget it," I sneered.

"So what's Miami like?" gushed Nina excitedly. "You think you're gonna like living there? I bet it's gorgeous there, isn't it?"

"Yeah," I agreed as Shard rubbed my breasts through my shirt.

"And speaking of gorgeous," continued Nina, "how is Shard doing? Is he still the finest thing walking?"

"Yeah, you know he is."

"I bet he's been all over you, huh?" asked Nina. "Have y'all knocked all the screws out of the headboard yet?"

Before I could respond, Shard murmured, "Tell your cousin I can hear every word she's saying. And tell her that the answer to that last question is 'no'; but it's about to go down real soon if she'll just hang up the phone." He had spoken loud enough for his voice to carry through the phone line.

Nina cracked up laughing. "Ohmygod! Why didn't you tell me that he was standing right there? Turn the volume down on the phone, girl."

"I think it's a little too late for that."

"Well," Nina let out a playful sigh, "I guess I better let you go. I don't want to hold up nothing."

"Wait. Tell Granny that I left Prince's little blue rattler in that diaper bag by the dresser. Sometimes that's the only thing that'll make him settle down. And tell her that—"

"It's all under control, Kyla. Prince has been fine for hours. He hasn't shed even one tear."

"He *hasn't*?" I asked, unable to hide the surprise in my voice. *My baby's not even missing me.* "Tell Granny to call me if she has trouble putting him to sleep. She can put the phone up to his ear so that I can talk to him. I think the sound of my voice comforts him."

"Yeah, yeah, yeah," said Nina. "Just go and enjoy your trip, okay?"

"Okay. Oh, and Nina, make sure that—"

Before I could complete my sentence, Shard reached out and pulled the phone from my hand. Then he pressed the button to power it off. "That's enough of that."

My mouth fell open in disbelief. "Shard, why'd you do that? I was trying to tell her—"

He just placed his hands on my hips and guided me around to face him. Then he began to kiss me so deeply and passionately, I felt my knees grow weak. It wasn't long before I had forgotten all about Nina and the conversation that we had been having.

Shard pushed me gently out of the kitchen and down the cool hallway, kissing me all the while. I had never craved anything as much as I craved him at that moment. All of a sudden, the memories of squeezing my pillow tight for one-hundred fifty nights came flooding back to me. My heart exploded with joy as I realized that in this exact space in time, I did not have to hug some inanimate object to soothe the pain deep inside of me. At this moment, I did not need some temporary emotional morphine. My morphine was right there in my arms.

He guided me back into his bedroom at the end of the passage.

I pushed him back onto the bed. "I missed you so much."

"I missed you, too."

I lifted my arms and stripped out of my tank.

"Look at you," he breathed as his eyes traveled down my smooth stomach. "You're so sexy."

"So are you." I helped him strip out of his own shirt and tank and swallowed hard at the sight of his still-beautiful body. In one fluid motion, I put one knee up on the bed, and then the other as I crawled over the mattress.

Shard laid back and welcomed me to his body with open arms. I placed my palms on the bed for support as I lay atop him. We began to kiss again, this time deeper and harder. We were both shirtless, so our bare chests were pressed together divinely. I enjoyed the way his hands felt as they caressed my back.

"You know, my mom used to have this doll that she loved," he suddenly revealed as he stared into my eyes. "Her dad was in the military, and he had been stationed in South America for a while. He sent her that doll from there, and she kept it until she was grown. She had it on the table right by her bed. It had this deep dimple in its chin, just like yours." He kissed my chin right on the spot where my dimple dented the skin. "Every time I look at you, I remember my mom's doll. She had hers, and you're mine."

"I'm *so* in love with you," I told him.

"Don't tell me how you feel," he whispered. "Just show me." He closed his eyes as I kissed him softly on his lips, his nose, his chin and forehead. I trailed my fingertips over his stomach, admiring its tone and definition. I quickly undressed and let his hands get reacquainted with me as well. When our bodies finally connected, I had to close my eyes to keep the tears from spilling again. It felt like I had finally returned home from a long and treacherous journey.

Shard and I spent the evening making love like we had never made love before. When we were finally spent, we took an hour to lie there and recuperate.

That night, he took me out on the town, giving me the opportunity to see Miami at its best. I had never seen so much diversity in any one place. The entire city was a medley of scents, sights, and sounds. Shard seemed right at home here. I noticed the comfort that he enjoyed as he cruised the streets, reclined back in the driver's seat of his sleek, black Jaguar. Everything that I laid my eyes on seemed to possess its own unique beauty—the vegetation, the landscape, the architecture. Even the women.

The members of the "fairer sex" were like the contents of a candy store with skin tones that could have represented everything from vanilla wafers, lemon drops, and butterscotches, to caramels, toffees, and milk chocolates. We saw them walking along the avenues, window-shopping, and sitting out at the sidewalk cafes in groups of twos and threes. The sizzling weather had forced them to don their scantiest attire, so they were revealing more flesh than I had ever seen during the summers in

St. Louis. I was disturbed by the fact that Shard had been living here among this abundance of beauties for so many months. I immediately began to wonder if he had been seeing other women while we had been apart.

"Do you really like it here?" I posed as I turned in the passenger seat to look at him.

"Yeah, I do. And what do you think so far?"

"It's cool. But I can't help but think that I'll probably miss St. Louis. Do you ever get homesick? Don't you miss the house in Chesterfield?"

"Life goes on. There's nothing left there for me. My folks are locked up, and my crew has jumped ship. I don't have any ties to St. Louis or East St. Louis anymore."

"You have me and Prince," I said pointedly.

He looked at me. "You know I didn't mean it like that."

I sat back in my seat and tried to ignore the troubling feeling his words had given me.

When we got home, I immediately stripped out of my dress and stepped underneath the warm spray of the shower. After washing my body and hair, I dug into Shard's dresser drawer and found an old East High School practice jersey, which I pulled on over my simple white cotton panties. By the time I climbed between the cool sheets, I realized that I was exhausted. I turned over onto my side and faced the large window that looked out over the city. I began to wonder what Prince was doing. I missed him so much it was almost like a physical pain. How ironic. Even though I was there with Shard, I still felt empty. I was still unfulfilled. I had *never* felt unfulfilled before when Shard and I had been together.

I relaxed a bit as I felt him slide into bed next to me. I waited to feel him wrap his arms around me and hold me, but he didn't. When I turned my head to look at him, I saw that he was lying on his stomach, his face turned in the opposite direction. I stared at the back of his head for a long time, listening to the sound of his heavy, even breathing.

Three years ago, this scene had merely been a dream that I could not have fathomed would someday come true. Here I was, sharing Rashard Phaylon's bed, watching him while he slept. Three years ago, this had been my ultimate fantasy. So why didn't it feel so fantastic anymore?

I told myself that I was only tripping because I was missing my son. Once we were all together, everything would go back to normal. Then I sighed wistfully as I realized that I didn't even know what "normal" meant for us.

When I opened my eyes the next morning, I wasn't surprised to find Shard's side of the bed empty. I stretched, and then headed to the adjacent bathroom to wash my face and brush my teeth. Later, as I padded down the hallway to the bright, sun-filled kitchen, the tantalizing aroma of an exotic breakfast greeted my nostrils. I grinned with surprise when I rounded the door frame and spotted the spread that Shard had set up on the black pub table. It looked like a scene out of *Metropolitan Home* magazine. The table had been set for two and was laid out with a platter of ultrathin rolled crepes sprinkled with powdered sugar, a bowl of fresh sliced pineapples, and a steaming hot potato and cheese frittata.

Shard was standing at one of the three floor-to-ceiling windows that lined the west wall, gazing out at the city's early morning activities. He was dressed in a pair of loose, baggy blue sweatpants, and an extra-large cotton tee. He clutched a bottle of water in one hand while he used the other hand to hold his cell phone up to his ear. I crossed the room and eased up behind him. He didn't seem the least bit startled when I wrapped my arms around his waist and planted a kiss on his back. He turned and offered me an easygoing half smile.

"Ah-ight, man," he was saying into the mouthpiece of his phone. "If I'm not here when you get to this side, Kyla will probably be around." As he listened to his caller's response, his eyes swept slowly and appreciatively over my bare thighs and legs. He watched as I sat and helped myself to breakfast. As soon as he had ended his call, he joined me at the table.

I savored a delectable forkful of the frittata. "Mmm. Where'd you get this?"

"I had it delivered from this spot down by the beach." He watched me silently for a moment. "So how'd you sleep last night?"

"Okay, but I kept waking up every couple of hours thinking about Prince. I was worried that he wouldn't sleep too good without me." I blotted my mouth with a napkin and reached across the table. "I need to check on him. Let me see your phone."

"It's still early. It's only like eight-thirty back in St. Louis."

"Prince is always the first one in the house to wake up.

He's probably screaming his head off right now because he does-n't see me lying there beside him."

"Nah, he's probably laid up in your granny's arms suck-ing a bottle without a care in the world. Give the kid a break. It's not good to get so attached."

"I'm his mother—I'm *supposed* to be attached," I replied with an uncomfortable chuckle. Shard seemed reluctant to hand his phone over to me, but he placed it in my outstretched palm. I dialed Granny's number and waited as the extension rang.

"Hello?"

"Hey, Granny. How are you?"

"I'm fine," she said tartly. "I guess you weren't planning to call and let me know that you had a safe trip."

"Nina knew that everything was fine. She was there at the house when I called to tell her that I had landed yesterday."

"Nina's not the one who's looking after Prince while you're gone. You could have had the courtesy to call me or Jazz and let us know something."

"How is my child?" I decided to ignore her little spill.

"He's doing good. After I gave him a bath and brushed his hair, he drifted right off. He slept all night."

"Good. Kiss him for me. I'll be calling again later to make sure he's still doing okay."

"He's with family, Kyla. He'll be just fine. So whatever you decide you want to do, then you go on and do it because Prince is gonna be taken care of." She hung up before I could say another word. Stunned, I pulled the receiver from my ear and stared at it as if it would explain the strange exchange. Finally, I looked at Shard.

"That woman is crazy," I declared, shaking my head.

"What'd she say?"

I looked at the receiver again, still trying to regroup. "She just said something about Prince being taken care of, no matter what I do. What the hell is that supposed to mean?"

Shard shrugged as he stood to his feet and rounded the table. "Who knows?" He placed his hands on my shoulders and kneaded his fingers into them until I was completely relaxed. I closed my eyes and lost myself in his touch. "So, listen," he added. "We got a big night tomorrow. Mal's cousin Rob is expanding one of his businesses, and he's having a white affair out at The Pavilion Ballroom to celebrate. We need to be there."

I looked back at him. "We have to go out tomorrow? Baby, I don't really want to mingle while I'm here. I thought that we would just stay in and keep each other company. I'm just not in the mood for the crowds and the noise."

"Come on. This is a big night for my partner. I need to at least show up at the spot. We'll just go for an hour or two, and then we can leave, ah-ight?"

"I didn't bring anything nice enough to wear to a white affair," I protested in a last-ditch effort to talk him out of the planned event.

"I'll buy you something. So why don't you go ahead and finish breakfast. While you're doing that, I'm gonna run down to the barbershop and then stop by the carwash. When I get back, I'll take you shopping. I want you looking extra-hot so I can show you off tomorrow night, ah-ight?"

"Okay."

"Oh, yeah," he added before he made his exit, "Mal is gonna stop by with some game tickets he copped last night. He usually just walks in, so don't let him catch you off guard."

As soon as Shard left, I pulled on a pair of jeans and a tee and began to tidy up. I raked our leftovers into the garbage disposal and then washed the dishes. When the kitchen had been returned to its former glory, I headed into the bedroom to tackle the mess we had made there the previous afternoon and night. I decided to strip the sheets and pillowcases from the bed and toss them into the washer. The top sheet was easy to remove, but the fitted sheet posed quite a challenge. The California king-sized was not light work for one person.

I wedged my hand underneath the mattress and worked to free the elastic rim of the sheet. It was such a snug fit I had to raise a corner of the mattress to get a better grip. It was too heavy, though, and it soon fell back to the box spring, just barely missing my fingers. Frustrated, I used all of my weight to push the mattress toward the opposite wall. Once there was space between it and the frame, I was able to finally remove the sheet. I gathered the bedclothes in my arms and carried them to the nook off the kitchen where the washer and dryer were housed.

Once I had a load swirling in the machine, I returned to the bedroom. I had bent to retrieve Shard's and my discarded clothing from the floor when I spotted the top half of a large white rectangular envelope jutting from between the mattress and the box spring. Realizing that I had worked it free while trying to strip the sheets, I pulled it out.

I had no intention of opening it or examining its contents, but as I started to wedge it back underneath the bed, the words typed on its surface made my hands freeze.

It was addressed to Rashard Phaylon, and it had been delivered from the Dade County Circuit Court. I flipped the envelope over and saw that it had already been opened.

Why was Shard keeping official mail underneath his bed?

More importantly, why was he even receiving mail from the courts in Miami?

Suddenly, I was overwhelmed by that unexplainable feeling again. That feeling of utter dread, doom, and uncertainty. I wanted to shove the envelope back under that bed, walk away, and convince myself that I had never seen it, but I couldn't. I just couldn't.

I lifted the unsealed flap and reached inside. My fingers found and produced a sheaf of papers that appeared to have been folded, and then unfolded prior to being placed inside the envelope. I swallowed the thick lump in my throat as I scanned the five words that were centered across the top of the first page: *Certificate of Dissolution of Marriage.*

My stomach flip-flopped as my eyes sped across the page. Printed in a space labeled "wife" was the name "Alejandra Castillo-Phaylon." Just above that, in the space provided for "husband," was the name "Rashard Phaylon."

I didn't understand what I was reading. Maybe my knowledge was limited, or maybe I just couldn't wrap my mind around the fact that Shard was listed as another woman's husband on a legal document. It literally felt like all the wind had been knocked right out of my body. I sank to my knees, still clutching the papers as I read and reread the information. According to the document, Alejandra was the "court petitioner," while Shard was the "respondent." The dissolution of marriage had been caused by "irreconcilable differences," and the union was "irretrievably broken."

The legal mumbo-jumbo was making my head swim. I must have sat there just staring at the papers for over half an hour. I didn't even hear Mal when he entered the condo. I was only vaguely aware of his voice in the next room calling out to me.

"Kyla? *Kyla?*"

I looked up just as he stuck his head around the door frame.

"What's up, baby girl?"

One look at my face, and his smile instantly faded.

"Who is Alejandra?" I demanded.

"What are you talking about?" stammered Mal. He eyed the papers in my hand, and then returned his gaze to me.

I stood and walked up to him, thrusting the papers roughly at him. "What is this all about? What does this shit mean?"

"I don't know." He stared at the documents as if the concept of words written on paper was completely foreign to him. "Where did you get these?"

"From under Shard's bed." I was gasping for breath.

"They were addressed to him. They have his name on them. Don't tell me that you don't know what they mean, Mal." I referred back to the words headlined on the top page. "What is dis ... dis ... dissolution of marriage?"

"I don't know." He couldn't even look into my eyes as the weak reply fell flatly in the air. He took a couple of steps back. "I'm leaving those tickets on the kitchen counter. Tell Shard I'll get up with him later."

"Wait!" I rushed to follow him, but he kept walking without even glancing back at me. "Mal, wait." My words seemed to fall on deaf ears. I followed him out to the paved driveway. "Don't leave me here like this," I cried in desperation as he pulled his car door open. "I just need some answers. *Please.*"

Mal paused with his hand on the door handle. He looked at me and sighed softly. "That's between you and Shard, baby girl. I can't involve myself in that."

"You can't involve yourself? You've been a part of all his shit since the day I met him, and now you tell me you can't involve yourself?"

When he didn't respond, I waved the papers at him again. "*Who* is Alejandra?"

He was silent, but I could clearly see how torn he was at that moment. He was torn between his lifelong kinship with Shard, and the unexpected friendship that had developed between me and him over the past few years.

"Forget it." I spun on my heels and headed back to the condo. "There's an address on these papers. I'll just go find out for myself."

"*What*? You can't be for real. You don't know a damn thing about this city. You don't know where you're going, or what you'll find when you get there."

"Hopefully, I'll find the fuckin' truth!" I screamed, whirling around to face him again. "Nobody seems to want to give me that anymore, so maybe I need to just take it upon myself to go out and get it."

"Kyla, don't go out there and get into some shit that you won't be able to get out of."

"I'm already in some shit that I can't get out of."

Mal looked back toward the street as if he expected Shard to come driving up at any moment. Then he looked at me again. "Get in the car," he reluctantly commanded.

"Why?"

"Just do it, Kyla, before I change my mind."

I walked to the waiting Cadillac and climbed into the passenger seat as Mal walked briskly up to the front door of the condo and pulled it closed. Then he headed back to the car and slid into the driver's seat. "I'm only doing this because I don't want you to go out there by yourself." Mal backed out of the driveway. "But I'm not condoning this. I think you should just wait and talk to Shard."

"Why? So he can feed me the same BS he's been feeding me since we've been together? All I ever get is *his* side of the story. Maybe that's why I never get to the bottom of anything. I think it's about time I started hearing somebody else's take."

Mal didn't argue with me. I settled back in the Cadillac

and studied the crystal clear blue sky through the sunroof as we whizzed through Greater Miami. My mind was racing, but I couldn't distinguish one thought from another. I didn't know how I felt. I didn't know what I expected. I didn't know what I hoped to discover. All I knew was that I had lived in the shadows of Shard's life for too long. I was ready to be brought into the light.

About fifteen minutes later, Mal and I were cruising through a clean residential neighborhood dotted with white-washed villas and gigantic coconut palm trees and princess palms. We turned onto a street called Upland Drive and slowed to a halt by the curb at one of the Mediterranean-style dwellings.

"You sure you wanna do this?" Mal asked as he killed the engine and stared at me.

"Yeah," I said bravely, though I didn't even fully realized what "this" was.

Mal took a deep breath and pushed his door open. "Come on." He gestured for me to follow him. I climbed out and trailed him up the sloping concrete drive. A carport was affixed to the side of the house, and a silver Lexus coupe was parked there. A purple and white girl's bicycle leaned against the wall. It had a banana seat and white handlebars. It reminded me of one I'd had when I was about seven years old. Mal walked up to the rust-colored front door and pressed the doorbell. Then he apprehensively stucked his hands in his pockets while he waited for a response.

I wondered where we were and why we had come here. It was obvious that this home and the person who resided in it were somehow connected to the documents I was still clutching in my sweaty palm. I had parted my lips a dozen different times during the ride over to ask Mal where we were headed, but the question had always gotten stuck on the roof of my mouth. The suspense was like a slow, thick poison coursing through my veins. I watched the door like a hawk as Mal finally reached out and pressed the bell again. This time I swallowed hard when I heard the deadbolt slide back with a click. The knob turned, and the door slowly opened. My breath caught in my throat as my pupils adjusted to the dim lighting inside the house. A cool air-conditioned breeze gusted out, bringing the aromatic scent of incense with it.

My eyes fell to the angelic form of a little girl, about seven or eight years old. She had a slim, oval-shaped face with golden skin that hinted on sienna. Her hair tumbled past her shoulders in ripples of glossy raven waves. Her eyes were almond-shaped and crowned with the lush brows and lashes that I had seen on only three other people in my lifetime: Maxwell Phaylon, Shard, and my son, Prince.

When the beautiful child saw Mal, her eyes took on an adoring light that probably melted his heart.

"Uncle Mal!" she squealed, jumping into his arms. "Uncle Mal!"

Mal laughed loudly and wrapped her up in a bear hug. "How's my lil' girl doing? How many kisses you got for me today?"

"Umm, three," she declared with a giggle. "One," she sang out, planting her little glossed mouth on his forehead.

"Two," she counted, placing the second kiss on his right cheek. "And three," she finished, posting the final one on his left cheek.

As they laughed together, my eyes filled with stinging tears. I had never seen this child, yet I knew exactly who she was. I felt so dizzy at that moment, I could barely see straight.

"Gabriela," a throaty female voice suddenly called. "What have I told you about opening the door when I'm not in the room?"

I looked up to see a stunning woman appear at the doorway.

"Do you know how dangerous that is, *mija*?"

"*Mami*, it's only Uncle Mal," Gabriela protested.

"Don't sass me," the woman warned. She reached out and protectively gathered the girl in her arms, breaking the hold she'd had on Mal. "Go into your room."

"But—"

"*Now*, Gabriela."

Gabriela sighed and waved good-bye to Mal before she turned and retreated into the shadows of the house. The woman walked up to the door where we stood and honed in on Mal. She was probably one of the most beautiful women I had ever laid my eyes on. I studied her creamy butterscotch-colored skin, her high cheekbones, and heavy, black, waist-length hair. The beauty mark that sat to the right of her full mouth gave her face an unintentionally seductive look. She was about my height, lean in the middle, and curvaceous in the hips. She looked to be about twenty-five or twenty-six at the most.

"Hi, Malcolm," she greeted him.

"What's up?" he returned. "I'm sorry for just dropping by on you like this. Did we catch you at a bad time?"

Her dark eyes darted from him to me, and then back to him again. "Who's she?" she asked, nodding in my direction.

Mal turned and gestured for me to come forth. I came only two steps closer.

"This is Kyla, Shard's girl," he informed her. He looked back at me. "And Kyla," he declared with a burden-laden sigh. "This is Alejandra, Shard's ex-wife."

Eleven

It was only after Mal introduced her as Shard's *ex*-wife that it occurred to me that I was clutching their divorce papers in my hand. Alejandra and I stared silently at one another until Mal spoke again.

"Kyla just wanted to meet you," he told Alejandra. "She didn't come to make trouble for you, ah-ight?"

I was surprised when she nodded her head. "Yeah, all right."

"I'll wait for you out here in the car," Mal murmured to me before he turned and headed back down the driveway.

Alejandra pulled the door open wider and stepped aside to allow me room to enter. "Come on in." I entered her home, tears belatedly falling from my eyes. I don't know if Alejandra didn't notice them or just chose to ignore them.

"Have a seat." She waved toward the huge gray couch that dominated the living room. I made my way to it and perched on the edge, gazing around at the plush gray carpet, the black-and-white oil paintings, and the big television against the far wall. I wondered how many days and nights my Shard had spent here, in this very room.

"Do you know me?" I blurted out as she sat right next to me and studied my face.

"I know of you. You're the one he's got the baby with, right?"

"He told you about me?"

"No, but Shard and I know a lot of the same people, so … word eventually gets around."

"He *never* told me about you," I said. "We've been together for three years … He never told me."

"That doesn't surprise me," she said softly. She cocked her head to the side and stared thoughtfully at me. "Does he even know that Malcolm brought you here?"

"No. I was cleaning up this morning while he was gone, and I found these papers. I had to know what they were all about."

She gazed at the documents, and nodded. "We just finalized the divorce." She said this as if that statement alone would answer all of my questions.

"How long were you married?" I demanded.

"Almost eight years."

My whole body went numb.

"About two years into it, he got restless, though," she explained. "He left me and went back to St. Louis. We were separated for so long, it felt like divorce anyway. I just took the initiative and made it legit."

"How old is your daughter?"

"She's seven. She barely even knows her *papi*. Shard is almost like a stranger to her. He sends Malcolm by here with the child support and the birthday and Christmas gifts." She shook her head. "He lives like fifteen, twenty minutes away, but he can't even take the time to stop by and see how she's doing. He's a telephone-daddy. A couple phone calls a week is all the quality time she gets from him."

I began to wonder why Alejandra was so willing to share her business with me. She didn't even know me. It occurred to me that she could still be in love with Shard. Perhaps she was only trying to sabotage my relationship with him by telling me these things.

As if on cue, Mal rapped on the door and pushed it open an inch. "Ay, Kyla, I think we need to cut this short." Before I could reply, he had closed the door again.

I looked at Alejandra. There was still so much I needed to know from her. "I appreciate you for talking to me," I said.

"No problem."

We both stood to our feet. Just as we reached the door, I turned and looked at her. "Can I see your daughter again?"

Alejandra hesitated, but slowly looked back over her shoulder. "Gabby? Come here, *mija*."

A few seconds later, the adorable child rounded the bend

and reappeared in the living room. She looked at her mother and me with wide-eyed curiosity.

Alejandra bent and scooped her up in her arms. "Oh, *mija*, you are getting so heavy," Alejandra groaned. "Can you say hi to Miss Kyla?"

"Hi," Gabriela said shyly with a sweet little wave.

"Hi," I returned.

I drank her facial features in, knowing beyond a shadow of a doubt that she was Shard's child. The full lips and the rich, slanted dark eyes were all the proof that I needed. I quickly turned away from them before they could see the fresh tears that had sprung up in my eyes. I was too choked up to even say good-bye. I pulled the door open and rushed out of the house, back down the paved driveway.

Mal was perched on the hood of his car, holding his phone up to his ear. He was just ending a call when he looked up and saw me. The expression on his face told me that Shard already knew about my spur-of-the-moment visit with Alejandra.

"I had to tell him," said Mal. "I got caught up in this shit, so I felt it was only right that I tell him what was going down."

When I didn't reply, he rounded the car and caught my arm. "You alright?" He stared into my eyes with the same compassion and concern that he had always shown me.

"Yeah." The new tears broke free and zigzagged down my face. "That was just kind of heavy, you know? That's a lot to take in at one time like this."

Mal nodded with understanding. "I know." He helped

me into the car and then jogged around to the driver's seat. We rode back to Coconut Grove in complete silence. When we pulled up at Shard's condo, the Jag was parked there in the drive. Mal peered out of the window, and then focused on me. "I'm sorry about all this, Kyla," he said sincerely.

The way he said those words made me study him closer. There seemed to be a deeper meaning behind that statement. It seemed that he was apologizing for more than just the situation that had occurred this morning. I didn't question Mal, though. My battle wasn't with *him*. He owed me nothing.

I climbed out of the car and marched up to the front door. It wasn't locked, so I let myself in. The house was silent. All I heard was the quiet hum of the air-conditioning. I stepped through the foyer and paused on the threshold of the living room. There, I found Shard, pacing the floor like a caged animal. His dark eyes were mere slits. When he looked at me, I almost flinched. He had never looked so *livid*.

He stalked up to me, reached down, and violently snatched the papers from my hand. "What makes you think you have the right to go through my shit when I'm not here? This is *my* business. It ain't got a damn thing to do with you."

"*What*? How can you say that to me? If you don't believe that this has *everything* to do with me, you're crazy. I just met my son's sister, Shard—a sister that I didn't even know he had until an hour ago." I shook my head and stared at him. "How could you just act like she didn't exist? Is that the way you operate? You make babies and start families and just leave when you get tired of the routine?"

"Hell, no."

"Are you sure about that? Because the way you played them sounds a lot like the way you played me and Prince."

"I didn't play you and Prince. That was a completely different situation."

"How so?" I challenged

"Because Alejandra was *business.*"

"*Business*?"

He grew silent, and I suddenly realized that he had not intended to utter that last statement. As I watched him, I saw a brief look of remorse pass over his face.

"What do you mean by 'business'?" I asked.

He just shook his head. Then he turned and walked away from me.

"So that's it?" I followed him down the hallway to the bedroom. "That's all you have to say for yourself? You got an ex-wife, and a seven-year-old child that you never even *mentioned* to me, and you ain't got *nothing* else to say about it?"

"What do you want me to say? That I'm sorry? That I wish I had been there for my lil' girl? If I tell you all that, what is it gonna change? Like I said before, that situation doesn't concern you. And I'm not gonna apologize for some shit that went down before I even met you."

I slowly seated myself on the edge of the bed and stared up at him. "Did you love her?"

"What I had with her ended a long time ago."

"But you married her. You gave her a child. You must have loved her at some point. She said that you just got up and left one day." The tears began streaming down my face as I imagined how Alejandra must have felt when Shard had abandoned her.

"So do I have to sit around and worry about you getting up and leaving me again, too?"

"I can't even believe that you're asking me something like that."

"It's a fair question. If you did it to her, why wouldn't you do it to me?"

"Because you're not her, Kyla. You're not Alejandra. You're not Zaina, and you're not any of those other weak women I wasted my time on in the past."

His words surprised me. I bit my lip and gazed down at him as he squatted before me and held both my hands in his. "You never let other people come between us before," he said, softening his tone. "Are you gonna start doing that now? Are you gonna start doubting me and everything I'm trying to do to give you and Prince the life y'all deserve?"

"No."

I sincerely wanted to believe that Shard had our best interest at heart. I wanted to believe that my son and I were the most important things in his life, but for some reason, it was becoming harder to convince myself of that.

"Help me to understand all this," I implored. "Make me understand why you kept this hidden from me. You were married to another woman the whole time you were with me. You had a child that you denied to me. What am I supposed to think about all that?"

"You want me to make *you* understand?" He suddenly grew angry again. "How can I do that, when you didn't even try to see it from *my* point of view? You took it upon yourself to dig for that shit. You put Mal in the worst possible position, and you went to *my ex* instead of coming to me for answers. What made you think that she would keep it real with you?

"You got faith in her? You got three years of your life invested in her? Have you shared a home, and a bed, and a secret that you'll take to your grave with *her*?" When I didn't reply, he gripped my chin and burned my eyes with his. "That's what you have with *me*," he reminded me. "Ain't nobody gonna keep it realer with you than me. You remember that the next time you run to a bitch to get information about me."

"I'm sorry that I went behind your back," I sobbed, "but this whole thing has got me so shook, Shard. All I keep seeing is myself in *her* shoes a few years from now."

He sighed and shook his head. "Ah-ight, so tell me what I need to do to get you out of that frame of mind."

"You need to let me and Prince make this move as soon as possible. When I catch my flight back home Monday, I can just get him and we can be right back down here—permanently."

I sensed Shard's hesitation. "It won't work," he finally said. "I got a lot of irons in the fire right now, and I need my space while I bring it all together. Just bear with me a couple more months, ah-ight?" When I didn't reply, he reached out and swiped the damp tear trails from my face with his thumb. "I'm just trying to protect you." He took me in his arms and held me. "You believe that, don't you?"

My heart ached with disappointment as I realized that, once again, I was surrendering to his desires while I completely neglected my own.

"Yeah." I felt like the foolish teenager I always seemed to become in his presence. "I believe you."

That evening, Shard began to reintroduce me to the "good life." In the months that we had been apart, I had forgotten how it felt to be able to walk into a high-end shop, select everything I wanted, and walk out with all of it in my possession. I didn't know if it was Shard's desire to keep up appearances that fuelled his generosity, but I wondered why he was still acting as if money were no object. He just patiently sat back and scanned *The Miami Herald* while I tried on one designer garment after another in search of the perfect look for the event that we were attending the following evening. I tried to focus on the task at hand, but every time I would begin to feel somewhat excited about the unexpected shopping spree, that impeding dread would bring me down again. I just couldn't stop thinking about all of the events of the past few months, culminating in the discovery of Shard's other family. I knew that he sensed the tension and the uncertainty I was still feeling. He refused to address it, though. His tactic was to act as if nothing had ever happened this morning.

After I decided on a white satin Nicole Miller dress and silver strappy stilettos, Shard took me to a restaurant that overlooked one of the local beaches. There, we feasted on shrimp skewers, crab legs, and key lime pie for dessert.

"So tell me more about Mal's cousin," I posed after we

had finished our meal and were walking back to the car. "He must really be a boss around these parts. You told me that he hooked y'all up with the jobs at the dock, and the cars, and everything. Why is he so willing to help all of a sudden?"

"Rob is family," said Shard matter-of-factly. "Why wouldn't he wanna help?"

"I don't know too many cousins who would go all-out like he has for y'all, though. I mean, what's he getting out of the deal besides a warm feeling?"

Shard looked at me with a raised eyebrow. "He knows that we're good for it."

"Does he also know that y'all are ducking the Feds?"

"He knows what he needs to know." Shard was elusive as we climbed into the Jag and buckled our seat belts.

I reached across the car. "Let me see your phone so I can check on my baby," I said, changing the subject.

"How many times a day are you gonna do this?" He sounded slightly annoyed. "Don't you think that your folks would call you if anything was wrong?"

"I'm not supposed to sit around and wait on anybody to call me. He's *my* baby, and he's *my* responsibility. That's how it works when you're a parent. You've ain't never had to be one, so I wouldn't expect you to understand that."

I don't know why I made that statement. I hadn't planned it. Still, I couldn't deny that I had meant every word of it. Shard's fingers paused on the ignition switch. He stared at me silently for a moment. "Well, shit, I guess I know how you really feel now. You wanna tell me where all that came from?"

"Just forget it." I stared out the window, wondering why I was suddenly feeling so depressed again.

"I thought we were moving past all this bullshit and drama. We just went shopping, and had a real nice dinner. Why are you pulling the claws out on me?"

"I'm not," I softly denied.

Shard didn't push the issue. We were silent during the entire ride. By the time we pulled back up at the condo, the air between us had grown thick and heavy with unspoken hostility. I clutched my bags in my hands as I followed him up the drive and waited while he unlocked the door. To my surprise, he merely pushed it open and pulled his keys from the lock. He didn't even step inside.

"I got some errands to run," he told me. "I'll be back later."

Before I could attempt to respond, he had turned and walked away, leaving me standing in the doorway. I sighed softly and placed my bags on the floor so that I could close the door behind me. I had remembered seeing a cordless phone mounted on the kitchen wall, so I made a beeline for it. I rescued the receiver from the cradle and dialed Granny's house, remembering, as always, to block Shard's phone number first.

"Hello?"

I didn't know why, but for some reason, the sound of her voice soothed me.

"Hey, Granny. How're you doing?"

"I'm good. How are you, Kyla?"

I hesitated before answering. "Fiine." Tears sprang up in

my eyes before I could stop them, but I was determined not to break in front of my grandmother. "How is Prince?"

"Oh, he's fine. He's lying right here on my lap, staring up at me like a grown man."

As I laughed with her, the tears rushed down my cheeks and met underneath my chin. "I miss him so much."

"You okay?" Granny asked in a concerned voice.

"Yes ma'am, I'm fine." I wiped the tears with my hand. There was a brief lull in conversation.

"Kyla, baby, I know I was a little snappy with you this morning," she suddenly confessed. "I'm sorry about that. I just didn't want you to get up there and let Prince fall by the wayside. I don't want you to take your focus from him. Promise me you won't do that."

"I *swear* to you that I won't do that. He's all I've been thinking about since I got here. I can't wait to get back to him. I need him just as much as he needs me."

"Oh, child, you don't know how good it makes me feel to hear you say that." Granny's voice was filled with relief. "Twenty years ago, Camille took her focus from you, and *you* paid the price for that. I don't want to see you repeat that pattern with Prince."

Slowly I sat down on the kitchen floor and leaned back against the wall. I parted my lips to speak, but then closed them again. A part of me wanted to tell Granny everything that had happened since I'd arrived in Miami, but something held me back.

"So how is Shard?" she asked as if she were reading my

mind.

"He's good. Matter of fact, he's doing way better than I thought he was."

Granny waited patiently for me to say more.

"Things just … aren't quite the way I pictured them to be." I had hoped that she would press me for more information, but she didn't.

"I'm sure you'll figure things out," she said.

"I guess I will."

"Well, listen, baby, I have to go. It's time for Prince to be fed."

"Granny, will you—"

"Kiss him for you? Don't worry. I'm doing it right now."

I smiled and hung up the phone.

I spent the rest of the night by myself in Shard's condo. I grabbed a pillow and a spare blanket from the closet and made myself comfortable on the living-room couch. For a long time, I stared at reruns on the TV screen until I could no longer stand the noise. Then I used the remote to turn it off. I lay there in the dark for awhile, wide awake, and hugging the pillow as if it were a human being. Memories of all those long nights I had spent alone in Chesterfield created déjà vu. I remembered lying there in my darkened bedroom while I waited for Shard to come home to me.

It was well after midnight when I heard his key in the door. I lay still and just stared at the wall, listening as his footsteps echoed through the foyer and materialized in the living room. Then his movement ceased. It was probably at that moment that he realized that I was lying there on the couch. He lingered there a moment, waiting for me to give him a sign that I was still awake. I didn't make a sound, didn't even stir. After a few seconds, he walked away, probably assuming that I was asleep.

I didn't tell him any differently.

The next morning, I awoke to the sound of familiar voices drifting into the living room, where I had slept the entire night. I sat up and stretched, wincing from the stiffness in my joints, then tossed the blanket aside and stood unsteadily to my feet. Then I headed straight back to the bathroom to splash cold water onto my face and brush my teeth. When I entered the kitchen, I found Shard and Mal perched on barstools at the countertop, downing glasses of juice.

"Morning, Sleeping Beauty," Shard teased as I walked over to the refrigerator.

"Morning," I said softly. I gave Mal a little wave as I produced a bottle of water and headed back out of the room.

"Baby girl," Shard called before I had taken five steps down the passage.

"Yes?" I replied woodenly without turning to acknowledge him.

"Come here," he requested. I hesitated, but still turned and trudged back to the kitchen. I paused at the door. "Come here, girl." I narrowed the distance between us. Shard reached for me and pulled me up to him, securing his arms around my waist.

"Why you trying to act all shy?" He leaned forward and

pressed his lips into mine. Mal's eyes fell to his juice glass. I knew what Shard was doing. He was trying to prove to Mal that the previous day's events had not affected our relationship. Maybe he was trying to prove that to me and to himself as well. I don't know if anyone was convinced, though.

I walked out of the kitchen without a single word and sat on the couch again, staring at the TV when Mal came through the living room, preparing to make his exit.

"I'll see you later on tonight at The Pavilion, baby girl," he called to me.

I actually had forgotten all about the white affair that we were scheduled to attend that evening. After Mal was gone, Shard appeared in the room. He sat down next to me on the couch. I scooted away from him an inch, but kept my eyes trained on the TV. I could feel him watching me, but I refused to return his gaze. He placed a hand softly on my knee. I shrank away from his touch.

"What's the matter?" he asked.

"Nothing." I kept my eyes on the television.

"Listen, I know shit seems real crazy, and that nothing is making much sense to you right now. I can imagine how confused you're probably feeling. Regardless of all that, though, I need you to keep your faith in me. Just try to relax and enjoy yourself tonight. Don't make me feel like everything I'm doing is in vain." He reached up to move a lock of hair back from my face. "We're gonna have a good time. By the end of the night, you'll see things a lot clearer."

When I still said nothing, he tapped me on my thigh with

his fingers. "I need to go out and help Mal and Rob get some things squared away. But I'm taking you somewhere so you can just lay back and let somebody pamper you for a while. There's a hot spot down in South Beach to get massages, manicures, the whole nine yards. That sounds nice, right?"

I shook my head. "I don't really want to—"

"It'll be real good for you," he said, interrupting my protests. "You've been stressing. I don't like seeing you like this. I want my old Kyla back, and I think this is the way to make that happen." He stood to his feet and beckoned for me to follow suit. "So go ahead and get dressed. It's all about you today."

◊ ◊ ◊ ◊

Even though I wasn't open to Shard's idea initially, I had to admit to myself that I needed the experience. He took me to a posh spa called Regalia that overlooked the Atlantic. Once inside, he pressed a credit card into my palm and planted a kiss on my mouth. Then, he was gone. The staff treated me like royalty. A tall, slim, brown woman welcomed me and ushered me into a vast waiting room with azure blue walls, plush antique-white carpeting, and soft, recessed lighting. She led me to a Queen Anne chair, then briefly excused herself, only to return shortly with a flute of chilled Mimosa, which she presented to me.

"I take it you're here for the full treatment." She gave me an inviting smile.

"I guess I am."

I opened my hand and gazed down at the card that Shard had left with me. It was an American Express Platinum business expense card. In the years that we had been together, I must have seen a dozen different credit cards with his name on them. However, I had never known him to possess a business card. My hostess, who introduced herself as Charlotte, was more than happy to accept it. In fact, the mere sight of it seemed to energize her. While she made the necessary arrangements for me to get "the works," I entertained myself by watching the seemingly well-to-do female patrons enter and exit the establishment.

I was surprised to see girls who looked no older than sixteen or seventeen sashaying by with their ridiculously expensive shoes, clothes, and bags. The expressions on their faces reflected their attitudes: They believed themselves to be invincible. They believed that they would be forever young. Forever beautiful. I remembered when I had been just as unaware of my mortality as they seemed to be. I chuckled bitterly to myself as it occurred to me that I was watching those girls through the eyes of an old woman, when, in actuality, I was only a few years older than they were. It seemed like an eternity had passed, though, since I had sat on hard wooden bleachers to watch my high-school sweetheart sink a jump shot. Or stopped at my locker to chat with my girls between classes.

I was soon pulled out of my nostalgia by Charlotte, who had come to whisk me off to the paradise that she said awaited me just beyond the white double doors. My session began with a long soak in an ozonated Jacuzzi. After twenty minutes, a female attendant presented me with a soft white terry cloth robe, and then took me to a small room where she gave me a deep tissue massage. Afterwards, I was seated in the lavender-scented salon, where I was treated to a manicure, pedicure, shampoo, and roller set. I couldn't remember the last time I had been so relaxed and comfortable. I was actually disappointed when Felicia, my stylist, lifted the hood of my dryer and turned off the airflow.

By the time Shard came to pick me up, I was feeling like a new woman. I caught a glimpse of myself in one of the full-length mirrors that lined the reception area, and I was pleased by the glow of my skin and the sparkle in my eyes. While Shard signed the receipt, I fluffed my voluminous hair with my hands and watched it settle softly around my face and over my shoulders.

"So," he said as we headed out together, "you feeling somewhat mellowed out now?"

"Yeah, I am."

"Good. Just try to keep this vibe for me tonight. Let's do it big like we used to, ah-ight?"

He popped the locks to the Jag and opened my door for me. I sat down and looked up at him. He returned my stare. The look in his eyes tugged at the corners of my lips, threatening to pull a smile from them.

"Ah-ight." I finally agreed to his unspoken truce. "Let's do it."

I'd like to be modest, but I can't lie : Shard and I arrived at The Pavilion Ballroom that night looking like beautiful young *stars*.

I had not known what to expect, so I had been shocked when he had pulled up at the massive white Grecian-style building. The place was so ritzy it was even being serviced by valets.

As we walked up the steps of the entrance, I was wondering why we were coming to such an elegant spot. I mean, we had class, but considering Shard's chosen occupation, we didn't usually mingle with this particular level of society.

Nonetheless, we headed right up to the main doors, me in my divine white Nicole Miller, and he in a starched white Ferragamo dress shirt with barbell cuff links and ivory dress slacks. A uniformed doorman held the door open for us, and we sauntered into a space so large, our footsteps echoed from the marble floors and deflected off the walls. In the distance, I could hear the thump of music and the collective murmur of a large crowd. I followed Shard up a small flight of carpeted stairs. A quick turn, and we were walking into the ballroom.

As my eyes got adjusted to the dim lighting, I was pleasantly surprised at the gathering we found there. The room was filled with well-dressed, diverse urbanites. I looked around me and took note of men and women ranging from age twenty-five to about forty-five. They were mostly black, but there were a few Hispanics and whites sprinkled throughout the room. People were talking, laughing, and drinking. They all looked so comfortable and confident. It didn't feel like any other party I had ever been to.

I suddenly heard an animated male voice echo through the space.

"My man, Shard, is in the *building*!" he screeched as if Shard were a rock star or a hip-hop don. "What's going on, man?"

I followed the sound of the voice and discovered that it

was coming from the deejay's platform at the far end of the room. Shard raised his hand high to acknowledge the grinning man at the turntables.

"What's happenin', Shard?" guys greeted him as we strolled in. "How're you doin'?"

"I'm feeling beautiful, man," Shard replied as he gave them the traditional handshake-hug combination. Though the atmosphere was warm and inviting, I still felt a bit out of place. From force of habit, I moved closer to Shard and took hold of his hand for security.

He looked back and smiled at me, but pulled out of my grasp. "I have to go up here and holla at a couple'a people." He gave me a nudge toward the center of the room. "Why don't you mix it up a little bit? Have a drink."

"You know I don't drink."

"Yeah, and that's probably why you've been so uptight lately. Come here." He guided me to the bar, where a very dark man in a white dress shirt was pouring and serving up spirits. "Let her have an apple martini," Shard told him. The man nodded and went to work behind the counter. Seconds later, he passed me a glass that contained a neon-green-colored drink, garnished with a plump red cherry. I accepted it and took a sip just to appease Shard. My eyebrows shot up as I realized it was delicious.

Shard chuckled at my expression. "I knew you would like that. Just sip on it till I get back, ah-ight?"

I nodded in agreement as he made his way back through the crowd. Combing the room with my eyes, I searched for a place to sit. I soon spotted a section in back that had been set up with a few tables and chairs. As I made my way over, I had to wedge by pairs and groups, cloaked in white attire and engrossed in conversation. Some were discussing trifles like popular TV shows or the hottest new hangouts. Many, though, seemed to be focused on more pertinent issues, like the stock market and the recent boom in Miami tourism.

Once I had secured a chair, I sat down and placed my drink on the table that accompanied it. As I carefully observed the people, the overwhelming loneliness I had felt since arriving in Miami came crashing down on me again. I reached for my martini and took a healthy swig. It was so good, I took a third and then a fourth swig until my glass was completely empty. I scanned the room for Shard, but saw no sign of him. I was elated when I saw a white-jacketed attendant pass through, wielding a tray of glasses filled with golden champagne. I waved to him, and took one when he extended the tray to me.

I didn't know how well champagne mixed with martinis, but for some reason, it was becoming easier to knock back the alcohol. I drained the glass in no time and headed to the bar for a refill. I was working on my second champagne when Shard suddenly reappeared. He was smiling softly, and I noticed that his beautiful eyes were sparkling like the wine.

"Come here," was all he said to me as he took my hand in his. I followed him through the crowd and up the steps of the deejay's platform. There, we were elevated a few feet above the gathering. I looked out over the crowd, grateful that he had finally rescued me from the sea of strangers. As I looked around the large platform, I quickly saw why he was so mellow. There was an opened bottle of Moet on a nearby table. He grabbed it immediately and motioned for my half-empty glass. I started to shake my head, but he filled it up for me anyway.

"I think I've had enough." I leaned and swayed. "I feel kinda funny."

"That's because your body's not used to it. You'll be okay in a minute."

I shrugged and took a sip while he placed the bottle at his lips and began to guzzle it like soda. "We're gonna get messed up with these drinks." I giggled, not really understanding why my own statement had been so funny to me.

"I think you're already there," Shard declared with a laugh.

Just then, Mal emerged from the darkness and stepped up on the platform with us. He was dressed sharply in white linen pants and a short-sleeved white linen shirt. He and Shard engaged in their usual camaraderie, and then Mal turned to wrap me in a full hug and plant a soft kiss on my cheek. He was clutching a clear plastic cup filled with a brown beverage. His demeanor told me that it wasn't his first or even his second drink that evening. As I surveyed the crowd again, it dawned on me that almost everyone was nursing a beverage of some sort.

The deejay began to spin a classic slow R&B song. The room exploded with cheers, and the well-dressed men and women began to dance and move to the music. I had to admit that the song was just as intoxicating as the alcohol. Before I knew it, Shard had grabbed me from behind and was using his hands to guide my hips to the rhythm. I moved with more fluidity than I knew I possessed. Still sipping my champagne, I closed my eyes and grinded against him in the most erotic manner allowed in public.

"*Damn*, baby girl," proclaimed Mal, watching my sensual movements, "it's like *that*?"

"Man, it's *always* like this," Shard bragged to him. "You see why it's so hard for me to stay away, right? She knows *exactly* what I need."

I don't know why his declaration disturbed me so much, but it did. As usual, though, I didn't question him. I didn't want to ruin the relaxed mood. As soon as I finished off my champagne, Shard supplied me with a fresh glass. By then, I had lost count of the number I had downed. As the evening wore on, I grew more comfortable by the minute. When an old hip-hop track began to play, we followed the deejay's instructions to "throw our hands in the air and wave 'em like we just didn't care"—a phrase I hadn't heard in years.

It suddenly occurred to me that I was actually having fun. Then it also occurred to me that in the three years that we had been together, Shard and I had never gone out and had fun like this. Sure, we had gone to a hundred different parties and a thousand different clubs. Once there, though, we had always just taken our thrones as the golden couple. We had always been untouchable and inaccessible to anyone who wasn't down for Shard's cause. We had never *really* laughed together like this. We had been too focused on keeping up the image, pulling off the schemes, and dodging the drama.

Over the next few hours, I lowered my defenses completely. I giggled uncontrollably when Shard kidnapped the deejay's microphone and began to address the lively crowd.

"Y'all having a good time out there?" he called.

"Yeah!" they chorused.

Shard passed me the mic while he worked at popping the cork from the new bottle of Moet that a waiter had just brought to him.

"Hey, Shard," a male voice called from the floor, "we see you got the good stuff up there, while you got us drinking the domestic down here! What's up with that?"

The crowd laughed. Shard grabbed the mic from me.

"Damn, I hate ingrates," he fired at the culprit with a grin. "I'll just have my man over there to snatch your cup, and we'll see how fast some domestic Miami tap water will get your ass faded."

The crowd roared. I laughed along with them, resting my hand lightly on Shard's shoulder. I was surprised when he captured it and pulled me to the front of the stage.

"Ay, man, turn the music down for a second," he instructed the deejay, gesturing with his hand. I looked at Shard with a puzzled yet curious frown.

"On a serious note," he said into the mic, "I do wanna thank all you for supporting yet another venture, ah-ight? The past few years have been real good to me, and I owe a lot of my success to a lot of the people in this room."

My scowl deepened, and my half smile disappeared. I was totally confused by Shard's impromptu speech. I looked back at Mal, but he was watching the crowd.

"Almost everybody in here has contributed to my vision in some way or shape," Shard continued. "Some of you put in your money. Some put in time, and some of you put in a lot of energy. Whatever it was that you contributed, though, I hope you all saw a worthwhile return on your investment."

Applause rippled through the air. Shard then focused his attention on me.

"With all that being said, I want to introduce a very special and lovely young lady to you. I like to think of her as my *primary* investor. They say that behind every man is a good woman, and I think she's living proof of that. This is Ms. Kyla Brown."

Still clutching my hand, he used it to guide me in a slow turn, giving everyone an unobstructed view of me.

"What do you think, fellas?" he added.

The room erupted with hoots, howls, and catcalls as the men expressed their appreciation. I began to feel nauseous, and I knew that it had very little to do with my alcohol intake. I didn't understand what was happening around me. Nothing was making sense. How had these people contributed to Shard's life in any way? Furthermore, how had they done it for the past *few years*? I looked at Mal again to see if he was as confused as I was. He seemed to be working extra-hard to avoid my eyes, though.

The festivities resumed as Shard cued the deejay to start the music back up.

I tugged on his shirt sleeve. "We need to talk."

"Ah-ight. After we leave here."

He stepped back off the platform, leaving me to stand there and stare after him. I turned to Mal, but he was already shaking his head as I approached him.

"I'm not getting in this one, baby girl," he said firmly. He set his empty cup down on one of the four-foot speakers that lined the platform. Then he kissed me affectionately on the forehead. "Just in case I don't see you before you leave out tomorrow, you have a safe trip, okay? I'll holla at you and the baby when y'all make it back this way. Tell Shard I'm calling it a night." Then just like that, he was gone, too.

My head was now pounding, and the bass pulsating from the sound system was only making it worse. I made my way unsteadily to the floor, and then pushed rudely through the crowd in search of Shard. I was quickly sobering up, and now that my brain was beginning to work at normal capacity again, the unanswered questions it contained were threatening my sanity. I finally spotted Shard in a corner near the back of the ballroom, conversing with three other men. I walked right up to him and placed a hand on my hip.

"So which one of these guys is Rob?" I gestured toward his cohorts.

"What?" Though his face wore a smile, his eyes narrowed and were burning into mine.

"I said, *which one of these guys is Rob?*"

When he didn't respond, I turned to face the men. "Do either of y'all know somebody named Rob?"

They shook their heads in both uncertainty and confusion. I looked at Shard again, waiting for an explanation. He gave me none. I turned and stalked back up to the deejay's designated area. The doubts were ringing louder in my ears than the music as I grabbed the microphone from the startled disc jockey's hand.

"All right, listen up," I snapped into the mic. "Everybody listen the hell up."

My angry demands grabbed the attention of every living soul in the room. The chatter, laughter, and music once again came to halt. "Turn up the lights," I added to no one in particular. I waited impatiently as the ballroom's twelve crystal chandeliers glowed to life. As soon as I was able to look at each and every face, I spoke again.

"If there is anyone in this room by the name of Rob, I need him to step up, please."

People began to look around, curious to see "Rob" for themselves, and then to see what my business was with him. After thirty seconds of silence, though, no one had staked a claim on the name.

"So, there's no Rob here?" I asked.

When I still received no confirmation, I nodded my head knowingly.

"That's what I thought," I murmured into the microphone. I looked across the vast room at Shard, who was glowering at me. I pointed directly at him. "You're a lying son of a bitch." With that, I shoved the microphone back at the deejay, waded through the stunned crowd, and stalked out of The Pavilion Ballroom. All I heard was the sound of my solitary footsteps resounding over the marble floor and bouncing off the walls. Each step was like an exclamation of rage. I had just reached the exit when a strong hand seized my upper arm in a vicelike grip.

Shard forced me around to face him. "What was that shit all about? You just made me looked like a damned fool back there, Kyla."

"Yeah, well, welcome to my world. You've been making me look like a damned fool for the last three years."

"What are you talking about?"

"What's going on with you, Shard? What have you been doing down here?" I searched his eyes. "Tell me the truth. For God's sake, just *tell me the truth.*"

He sighed softly and clenched his jaw muscles.

"Hey, Shard, we'll see you next week," a guy called as he and three others headed for the exit. "Thanks for everything."

"Cool," Shard mumbled, giving them a half-hearted wave. I noticed that they were craning their necks, trying to watch us as they walked out.

"Come on." Shard pulled me outside and toward the parking lot. He used his remote to grant us access to the Jag. Once we were inside, he started the ignition and pulled out. We rode in silence for several minutes.

Finally, he rubbed his hand over his head and looked at me. "I was gonna tell you everything tonight. You didn't give me a chance."

"You've had plenty of chances. I've been here for three days, and I've been begging you to come clean with me. What am I supposed to think when I get here to find that you have a whole other family? What am I supposed to think when you take me into a room full of strangers who all know you by name? You're always pushing that 'no secrets, no lies' motto at me, but you're constantly keeping secrets from me and telling me lies. I want the truth, Shard. I don't want half of it, or part of it. I want the *whole* truth."

Shard had just pulled up in his drive. He shifted into park and killed the ignition. Then he looked deep into my eyes. "You're not woman enough to handle it."

"I been handling more in the past three years than most women could handle in a lifetime." I tried not to show how much his words had hurt me.

"Yeah," he cracked sarcastically, "you always handle shit like an adult, Kyla." He held out his left forearm to display the jagged scar that ran up to his elbow. "Which is why I damn near bled to death when you cut me last year, right?"

"That was an accident."

"That's not the point. You always flip out over shit. That's why I feel like I have to keep things from you. You're damn near twenty-one, and sometimes you still act the way you did when you were seventeen."

"So you're saying that I'm immature? Even though I handled your business for you in St. Louis while you were on the run? Even though I had your child prematurely, and worked to take care of him while you were chilling down here on the beach? All that, yet, *I'm* immature?"

"Who says I was chilling on the beach? Don't tell me what the hell I was doing, ah-ight? You don't know shit."

"You don't tell me shit!"

"Lower your voice, ah-ight?" he warned.

He pushed his car door open and stepped out. I climbed out, too, and followed him up to the front door. As soon as we were inside, I followed him to the kitchen. I was so infuriated by the fact that Shard was still skirting around the issue. He was still avoiding my questions and ignoring my concerns.

"Talk to me," I commanded as he opened the refrigerator and removed a bottle of water.

"What do you want me to say?"

"You can start by telling me who Rob is. Is he a drug dealer? Have you been down here slanging, Shard?"

"No."

"Well, who is he? Apparently, he's not this big-time business man that you and Mal claimed he was. He wasn't even at his own party."

Shard took his time unscrewing his bottle and taking a several gulps from it. Enraged, I stalked up to him, snatched the bottle from his hand, and flung it across the room.

"Who in the hell is Rob?"

Shard narrowed his eyes. "Ah-ight then. You want the truth, you got it."

I cocked my head to the side and folded my arms over my chest expectantly.

Shard gave me a superior smirk. "Rob doesn't exist," he said. "I made him up."

Thirteen

My mouth became sandpaper-dry. "What do you mean, 'you made him up'?"

Shard shrugged. "I knew that you were going to question me from the beginning," he explained. "I knew you would want me to explain why I chose to come to Miami. And I knew you would want to know how I was surviving down here all this time. Making up that Rob story was the only way that I knew to keep you off of my back."

"So what have you really been doing down here all these months?"

He shook his head and gazed at me. "Tell me something, Kyla. Did you really think that I wanted to spend the rest of my life pushing crack to fiends? Did you think I was gonna sit back and let this bullshit legal system suck me in the way it did my father and my brothers? I'm down for my family, but I would never go out the way they did. I decided that a long time ago."

He began to pace the length of the kitchen. "I never wanted to be a hustler," he said bitterly. "I was thrown into the game. I grew up around it, but I always promised my moms that I wouldn't follow my father's footsteps. I managed to stay out of the game for a long time—until my folks got busted."

"You told me this story before," I interrupted impatiently. "You told me that you had to hustle just to survive after your family got locked up."

"But it wasn't about survival," he said. "If it had been about survival, I would have put myself in a legit situation and came up off that. But when my folks went down, they still owed Eli all that money. My father was real messed up about it. It was a large debt, and there was nothing he could do to square it away behind bars. He started putting all this pressure on me. He told me that it was all in my hands because I was the only Phaylon still walking free. I couldn't say no. He's my father."

He sucked his teeth bitterly as he continued. "So I told him that I would do whatever it took to pay off his debts. The only condition was that he had to do whatever it took to help me get out of the game once it was done. He agreed to that. The first thing I did was line up my own connect. I never really felt too solid about Eli, so I headed down to Miami and cut my own deals. After that, I had to assemble a crew. Me and Mal had been best friends since like third grade, and I trusted him more than anybody else around me, so I brought him in on the scheme. He brought in Hutch and Shorty ... and just like that, we had the game on lock in St. Louis."

He shook his head. "I gotta admit, though, after a couple months, I started to see why it's so hard for some people to get out of the lifestyle. The money, the women, the power ... all that was addictive. I didn't want to lose sight of the real reason I was in it, so I started focusing on my plans for life *after* the game. With the type of money I was making, my father's debt could have been paid off in a year tops, but I decided to hold back on some of the profit. I didn't know what to do with it, though. I didn't know where to put it to keep federal eyes off me.

"Then one weekend, I came to Miami to meet up with my connect. While I was down here, I dropped by this bar on the beach. I was having a drink, and I started shooting the breeze with this old Cuban guy sitting next to me. Dude took a liking to me for some reason. We ended up playing some poker and basically getting drunk for the next couple hours. He invited me out to his house for dinner that night, so I took him up on it.

When I got there, I was blown away. The house was like a fuckin' palace. Dude had a vintage car collection, servants, the whole nine yards. I found out that the old man, Señor Castillo, was a tycoon down here. He had been a tobacco farmer, but had parlayed that into a cigar company that distributed worldwide. Then he had flipped the profit from that into a couple of restaurants and a resort hotel too."

Shard's eyes lit up with admiration. "I was fascinated by that old man. I wanted to be around him just to soak up the wisdom and to study the blueprint. He had more money than my father had ever touched, and he did it *legitimately*. That was amazing to me. I started taking regular trips here just to hang out with him. He had never had any sons of his own, and I guess he started seeing me in that light. His wife had died years ago, and the only family he had was his daughter—Alejandra."

The mention of Alejandra's name jolted me like an electric shock.

"So *that's* how you met her?" I asked softly.

He nodded. "I noticed that she had this thing for me. Whenever I would come around, I could see it in the way she looked at me. I mean, she was beautiful; but out of respect for her father, I never made any plays for her. But one day she called me, sounding all messed up. She told me that her father wasn't doing too well, and that she thought I should come down. I hopped a flight out here and found the old man in a real bad shape. Cancer was taking him out."

He cleared his throat. "I stayed there at the house with them for a few days. In that time, me and Alejandra talked a lot. She told me how scared she was to be alone. She told me how Señor Castillo was leaving her everything—the businesses, all the assets … everything. She didn't know anything about management, so she was planning to sell it all.

"The last night I was there, she came into my room and got in bed with me. Part of me wanted to stop it from happening, but there was this other part of me that just kept thinking about all the things she had told me. I kept thinking about her getting rid of the shit her father had built from scratch like that, and it was really killing me. The wheels in my head started turning, and

I figured that sleeping with her could work to my advantage. Señor Castillo was real big on keeping up appearances, and I knew that if Alejandra got pregnant before he died ..."

"He would want you to marry her," I finished for him.

Again he nodded. "And that was exactly what happened. It was like the chips fell perfectly for me. I got her pregnant, we got married, and five months later, the old man was gone. Alejandra had never wanted any part of the businesses anyway, so I took control of those. When she finally filed for divorce, she got some big-time lawyer, and I lost fifty percent of the ownership. I guess she just wanted to spite me because she ended up selling her half to some dude back in Cuba. She wouldn't let me buy her out."

He shrugged his shoulders nonchalantly. "It's cool, though, because dude she sold to is more like a silent partner. I call most of the shots. The businesses still provide me with a damn good living, and they also gave me a way to clean up all the dirty money I had made with Eli. I've been expanding and bringing in more employees and investors ever since. Our resort just signed a contract with a computer company to sponsor its annual convention for the next three years. That's what the celebration was all about."

"But I'm still so confused. The Feds ... don't you think that they'll eventually find you?"

"Feds won't catch me." Shard's confidence was unshakable.

"How do you know that?"

"Because," he said, "the Feds aren't after me. They never

were."

It felt like my heart had dropped out of my chest. "WHAT!? What the *hell* you mean they weren't after you!?"

"Pops had to hold up his end of the deal," said Shard. "After I paid Eli and did him a few favors, the debt was clear. My father's a smart man. He knew that the only way to really get me out of the game was to make people believe that I had lost the game. He knew a couple of crooked cops from his days on the streets. One of his old homeboys, Greg, is a retired detective, the same Greg that questioned you that day at the mall.

"He just went around the hood asking questions—just enough to make everybody think that I was being investigated. He even sent that fake connect to Eli, so that he would believe the connect had ratted me out. When I went AWOL, everybody figured that it had something to do with the cops being on my tail. Once niggas started coming to Booneville with the news that I was on the run, Pops knew that the job was done. That was why he called you out to give you that message. That was his way of telling me, 'mission accomplished.' It was a lovely camouflage. As close as you were to me, it even had *you* fooled."

"And Mal has been in on all this, too?" I inquired.

"Yeah. He was the only nigga that I trusted enough to share my piece of the pie with."

He stared at me, waiting for my reaction. I was in a state of shock, though. I *couldn't* react. At the moment, it was impossible. I just stood there for a full minute, staring back at him, trying to digest everything that he had told me. It was incredible. It was unbelievable. How could such an elaborate ruse have taken place right under my nose? How could I have been so blind? So naive? As the initial shock very slowly wore off, a veritable range of emotions began to wrack my mind and body. I felt deceived … angry … betrayed.

For three years, I had been a player in the strategic game that Shard and his father had been coaching. I had never been his queen. I had merely been one of his pawns. Feeling my knees wobble, I walked over to the table and seated myself weakly on a chair.

"So now you know," Shard murmured softly. "No more secrets. No more lies."

Shard's revelation left me spiritually and emotionally drained. After that, I took a long, hot shower and changed into a nightshirt. Then I perched dejectedly on the edge of the bed. I felt so empty. Even though Shard had given me an airtight alibi and explanation for his actions, something still felt unresolved. I couldn't quite pinpoint the issue, but it just kept gnawing away at my consciousness.

"So listen," Shard emerged from the bathroom freshly showered, donning white cotton pajama pants, "I was thinking that September would be a real good time for you and Prince to make the permanent move down here. The weather will be a little bit milder, and it'll make the transition smoother. What do you think?"

It amazed me the way that he could act as if he hadn't delivered life-altering news to me only hours earlier.

"Sounds good." I was still staring down at the comforter. He walked over to me, bending so that his lips were just inches from mine.

"I wish you didn't have to leave me tomorrow." He kissed my forehead, my nose, and finally my mouth. "But September's just around the corner. We'll be back together in no time."

He crawled atop me, silently urging me to scoot and lie back on the mattress. As my head met the pillow, I parted my legs and closed my eyes. I barely felt his lips when they met my neck and later found my stomach. Even though his hands were not cold, they did not warm and tingle my skin the way they always had before when he'd caressed me. When he entered me, I gasped from the physical discomfort I felt. It was like I was a virgin all over again. As he thrust back and forth, my eyes filled with hot tears that streamed down the side of my face.

"What's wrong?"

"Nothing," I whispered while the tears continued to fall.

Later that night, I stayed awake as Shard slept soundly. I perched on the large windowsill and gazed out at the night sky. One thousand different thoughts and questions were fighting for dominion over my brain. For the first time in my life, I could actually *feel* my soul warring with my body. I could feel my mind warring with my heart. I felt my flesh warring with my spirit. I hugged my knees to my chest while I searched the sky for answers. I didn't know what to do. I was still so confused by all that I had learned only hours earlier. I needed to talk to someone. But who? I certainly couldn't talk to my relatives. They would all be biased in their opinions of my situation. Usually, Shard was the person in whom I confided all of my fears and my pain. Who was I to confide in when *he* was the one who had caused such fear and pain?

"I'm so scared," I whispered as I stared at the sky. I didn't know who I was addressing. All I knew was that I desperately needed to unleash my emotions. The sky was so infinite, and so vast that in my heart of hearts, I knew that Somebody great and powerful had to have created it. If He who had fashioned stars and set them in that sky could have taken the time to fashion me and place me on the earth, then surely I could confide in Him.

"Can You tell me what to do? I'm so tired of hurting like this." I pressed my forehead against the cool windowpane and closed my eyes, meditating on that endless sky. "I don't know how to pray. I don't know if I'm doing this right. I don't even know if You can hear me right now." I sniffled softly and pressed my hand against the glass, too.

"But if You *can* hear me, then will You answer a question for me?"

I took a deep, shaky breath as fresh tears poured down my cheeks. "How do You know if somebody really loves You?" I shook my head against the glass. "I know You've been watching me. I know that You've seen everything that I've been a part of. Maybe I'm just wasting my time talking to You because You already decided that I don't deserve Your help. I know that a lot of my decisions were bad, but I swear that my intentions were good."

I clasped my hands together, interlocking my fingers. "So please ... show me what to do."

I looked over at Shard's body, stretched across the mattress. He was lying on his stomach, still sleeping soundly. The moonlight shined unusually bright through the window, illuminating his golden skin and black hair.

"Just show me what to do."

I sat and stared up at the sky for several more minutes. I heard nothing, saw nothing, and felt nothing. I sighed, curled up in the fetal position, and fell asleep right there on the windowsill.

Fourteen

I opened my eyes the next morning to the sound of raindrops splattering against the window. Slowly, I sat up and stretched the kinks from my muscles, then I padded to the night table. It was eight-fifteen, and my flight was leaving Miami International at five minutes after eleven.

I treaded over the cool, wooden floor in my bare feet, peering into every room in the condo. Shard was nowhere to be found. Upon returning to the bedroom, I gathered all of my belongings and packed them into my bags. Quickly, I padded into the bathroom and filled the bathtub with warm water, stripped off my nightshirt and underwear, and left them in a pile on the floor. Then I stepped into the tub and sank down until my chin touched the surface of the water. I lay my head back against the porcelain and stared up at the skylight overhead. Even though my heart was heavy, my head was surprisingly clear. All I could think about was getting home so that I could hold my baby. I wanted to smell him, kiss him, and tell him how much I loved him.

I looked up when I heard a short knock at the bathroom door. Before I could respond, the door inched open and Shard stepped into the room.

"Hey."

"Hey." I drew my knees up to my chin and stared at him.

"You feelin' ah-ight?"

I nodded. "Better."

"I ran out and grabbed some breakfast. Come and eat when you get out, okay?"

"Okay."

After breakfast, I finished dressing and peered out of the window to check the weather. It was still showering outside, but I was relieved to see that there was no indication of a storm.

"Did you get everything?" Shard asked me as he scanned the bedroom and bathroom for anything that I might have left.

"Yeah." I picked my bag up from the mattress. "I don't think I forgot anything."

Shard draped both of my bags over his shoulder.

"You'll say bye to Mal for me, right?" I asked him as we headed slowly through the condo and toward the front door.

"If you want me to. It's not like you're leaving for good, though. You'll be back in September. We'll barely have time to miss you."

"But still ... just tell him bye for me, okay?"

"Ah-ight. I can do that." He stopped short at the door. "Damn. It's raining harder out there. I guess we gotta make a run for it."

I nodded and pulled the hood of my Washington University sweatshirt over my head. Shard opened the door, and we rushed out to the waiting car. As soon as we were inside, I removed the hood. The cotton had gotten soaked, and my hair hung in damp ringlets. I shivered, even though the rain had been quite warm. Then I reached over to pull my seat belt down while Shard pulled out of the drive. I stared silently out of the window with my chin resting in my hand. The traffic was rather light, and we were halfway to the airport before I fully realized that we were even on the highway.

"You know you're gonna like it out here," Shard predicted as he turned the radio off. "Maybe when you come back, we could start looking for another place. Something bigger and more comfortable for a kid."

"Yeah. Maybe."

"There are some real nice houses around Coconut Grove. We don't really even have to stay in that area, though. If you want to, we could move out even closer to the beach. That would be cool, right?"

"Uh-huh," I absently agreed.

When he pulled into an empty space in a parking deck at Miami International, he cut the engine and settled back in his seat. Neither of us spoke or moved for several seconds. Finally, he turned to look at me. Instead of meeting his gaze, I peered out at the windshield wipers.

"You're so quiet," Shard finally noticed.

"I guess I just have a lot on my mind."

"I got something for you." He reached into one of the car's small storage compartments and produced a set of keys and dangled them before my eyes. I instantly recognized the diamond-encrusted charm in the shape of the letter "K" on the ring.

"My keys," I gasped and took them from his hand. "How did you get these?"

"I had Mal put the car in storage for you the day after I left. I couldn't let you ride around the 'hood in a Bimmer. It would have looked too suspicious. When you get back to St. Louis, though, you can go and pick it up, ah-ight? We'll make arrangements to get it down here in September."

"Where's the Rover?"

"I sold the Rover. The house, too."

"When?"

"One of my partners bought the Rover about a week after I left, and the house sold two months ago. Everything's good. Life in St. Louis is just memory for us now, baby girl. We have a clean slate."

I don't know what triggered my sudden moment of clarity, but in that instant, it all made perfect sense to me. The unanswered question that had been eating at me since the previous night finally spilled from my lips. "You weren't coming back for me, were you?"

"What?"

"You weren't coming back for me," I repeated, turning the question into a statement. "You used Alejandra to get those businesses, and you used me to pay off your debts and get all your money down here to you. You tossed her aside after she had served her purpose, and you were about to do the same thing to me."

"Hell, nah."

"Yes. I was right when I told you that her situation looked a lot like mine. That's because her situation *was* like mine, wasn't it?"

"No. It was totally different."

"Tell me how it was different!" I cried, incensed. "Tell me how I'm any different from Alejandra." I began to tick off on my fingers. "We were both young when we met you. We were both naïve. She sacrificed her daddy's fortune, and I sacrificed my whole damn life."

The more I spoke, the more it was revealed to me. It was like divine intervention.

"I didn't force you to sacrifice a damn thing," Shard argued. "I took care of you. I gave you a home and a family."

"I already had a family! I left my family because you made me feel like they didn't care about me ..."

My sentence trailed as I suddenly had another epiphany. "And speaking of my family, tell me what *really* happened between you and Jazz. You told me your whole devious-ass plan for Alejandra and her father, so tell me the plans you made for me and *my* family."

I saw the hesitation all over his face.

"Come on, Shard. I'm a big girl. I can take it. After all the shit you put me through, I can take anything now. Tell me how I fit into the story. You at least owe me *that*."

He still said nothing.

"You said Jazz seduced you, but that was a lie, wasn't it? You slept with her because you didn't want her to talk me out of being with you. You used that to keep her quiet for awhile, and then you finally told me because you knew I would take your side. You wanted to isolate me from my folks."

"That was the best thing I could have done for you," he hissed. "They had too much negative influence on you."

"Like you *didn't*?" The air grew thick with tense silence. "So why me? You had Zaina, and a hundred others girls ready to ride or die for you. What separated me from the rest of them?"

"Nothing, at first. But you always seemed to have something to prove. You wanted me, and you had to prove that you could get me. You got me, and you had to prove that you could keep me. You didn't want to be like your folks, so you had to prove that you were different. You had to prove that to them, to me, and to everybody else.

"I needed somebody like you in my life. Zaina was weak, and so were all those other girls I messed around with. They were cool for the little shit, but I needed a thorough chick by my side for all the major things I had in the works. You just kept proving yourself to me. You never seemed to have any limits. That was what I needed."

I winced at his declaration. "So you *used* me."

"We used each other. You loved the chase and the challenge I gave you. I loved the dedication and the loyalty you gave me. We were both happy, so what difference did it make in the end?"

"It made a difference because I *wasn't* happy. I've been very unhappy for a very long time; but I guess since you never really cared about me, it didn't matter anyway."

"I do care," he protested. "I didn't intend to fall for you the way I did, but when it happened, I was down for it."

"Which brings us back to my original question." I stared defiantly at him. "Were you planning to come back for me and Prince?"

"You know that Prince wasn't planned. Honestly, he wasn't."

"I guess that's my answer then. You never wanted any ties to bind you to me, did you? After my part in all this was over, you wanted to just walk away and leave me to try to pick up the pieces. Prince was the only thing that you *didn't* plan for."

When he didn't reply, I placed my palms at my forehead and sighed loudly. "How could I have been so fuckin' *stupid*?"

"Baby, you weren't stupid." He reached over to stroke my hair. "We both did some senseless shit, but we can't lose sight of everything we gained."

His last statement really struck a nerve with me for some reason. Right then, I felt an overwhelming desire to get as far away from him as humanly possible. I pulled the handle and pushed my door open, coldly informing him, "I have a flight to catch." Then I climbed out of the car, grabbed my duffels from the backseat, slammed the door, and trekked across the parking deck, dodging puddles along the way.

"Wait. Hold up," I heard Shard call as he jogged and caught up with me. He tugged my arm until I turned to face him. "You're not even gonna say bye to me?" He looked bewildered by my cold departure.

The rain had slowed a bit, but it was still falling hard enough to shock the senses. Shard didn't seem to notice or care, though.

"Don't just leave this shit to my imagination," he said. "Tell me what you're feeling."

He was gripping me so tightly it was as if his own life depended on it. It was then that I saw something glistening in his deep, dark eyes that I had never seen in them before. I saw fear.

I sucked my teeth and sneered at him. "I ain't feeling *nothing*."

In one swift and strong motion, I snatched my arm out of his grasp and briskly walked up to the automatic doors of the airport entrance.

"You ain't feeling *me*?" He followed me inside. "You ain't feeling *us*?"

I ignored him and kept walking.

"Answer me, dammit." He grabbed the hood of my sweatshirt and pulled me around to face him again.

"Get off me, Shard." I pushed him back. "You're gonna make me miss my flight."

"To hell with that flight. I need you to talk to me. Why you acting like this?"

"Like what?"

"Like you're not in this with me anymore."

"Apparently, I wasn't in this with you in the first place."

"We were always in this together," he stated softly. "I didn't like my life, Kyla. But I didn't sit around bitching and moaning about it. I just did what I had to do to change it. I can't believe you're resenting me for that."

I chuckled sarcastically and shook my head. "Don't even try it, Shard. It's not gonna work this time."

"What's not gonna work?"

"This sick little game you always play with me. Every time I start to wise up about you, you find some way to make yourself the victim and make me the bad guy. I'm not falling for it this time. Nice try, though."

I expected him to deny my accusations. I was surprised when he sighed softly and ran his hands over his head. "Okay, okay. I'm sorry. I'm not trying to insult your intelligence, ah-ight? I'll keep it real with you. Maybe I *wasn't* coming back for you at first. Maybe I did use you to get where I was trying to go. Once you had wired all my money to me without rousing suspicion, my plan was to just cut you loose. I admit that I was wrong for that. But it all backfired on me because once I got here, I was miserable without you.

"I kept trying to forget about me and you, but I couldn't do that. Life just seems so much easier when I'm with you." He rubbed his hand over his head. "I mean, you hold me down. Maybe I never really told you that, but you do."

Those words pushed the last bit of doubt from my mind. I knew then with absolute certainty what I needed to do. I pressed the keys that he had given me in the car into his free palm. He was so stunned he loosened his grip on me. "What's this supposed to mean?" He held the keys out in his outstretched hand as if they were foreign to him.

I took a couple of steps backward. "It means," I said in a firm, unwavering voice, "that me and you … are *over*."

A look of absolute disbelief clouded his face. He swallowed hard and bit down on his bottom lip. As he struggled to keep his composure, I turned and headed determinedly in the opposite direction. Shard caught me again, though, this time securing one arm across my chest and the other around my waist.

"Ah-ight, listen," he breathed in my ear.

I could hear the desperation in his voice.

"I can stand here all day and try to justify everything to clear my conscience; but the truth is, I just don't wanna lose you."

I heard him sigh softly with relief as I turned to face him.

"It's not about what *you* want anymore," I told him.

I had never seen him look so unsure of his next move. It was the first time any situation had ever been beyond Shard's control.

"I can't keep apologizing for what I did, Kyla. I had to look out for me."

"I know you did. So you should understand why I have to do the same thing."

I narrowed the space between us and planted a firm, final kiss on his mouth. When I pulled away, I saw the pain behind his mask of indifference.

"Bye, Shard."

I began to walk away for the third time. As I lost myself in the swarm of people bustling to and from their respective destinations, I half-expected him to once again intercept me and try to plead his case. With each uninterrupted step I took, my movements slowed, but I kept walking. It was only after I had checked my bags and moved out of the line that I dared to look over my shoulder. I stood on my tiptoes and craned my neck to see through the crowd.

Shard had vanished.

I made my way to the restroom that I had spotted on the other side of the counter. Once inside, I splashed two handfuls of cold water on my face, tore a rectangle from the roll of hard brown paper towels in the dispenser, and patted my skin dry. Then I leaned heavily on the sink and gazed at my reflection in the mirror. I looked weary but victorious.

As I exited the restroom, I fished some change from a pocket in my bag and stopped at the bank of payphones just outside of the door, where I lifted the shiny black receiver from the nearest phone and deposited several coins. My heart thudded in my chest as I listened to the phone ring.

"Hello?"

"Hey, Granny."

"Kyla? Hey, sweetie. Where are you?"

"Still in Miami at the airport. My flight will be leaving here soon. How's my baby?"

Before Granny could even reply, I heard the familiar

sounds of Prince's gurgles and coos in the background. I grinned, ignoring the tears that had gathered in my eyes moments earlier and were now rolling down my cheeks.

"I can't wait to get back to him," I declared. "Just a few more hours …"

"So you *are* coming back home?"

"Yes. Why wouldn't I be?"

"What time should I be at Lambert to pick you up?" she inquired, ignoring my question.

"About one o'clock."

"I'll be there."

"Thanks." As I started the hang up, I heard her call out to me.

"And Kyla?"

I placed the receiver at my ear again. "Ma'am?"

"I love you."

"I love you, too, Granny."

Thirty minutes later, I was seated on American Airlines, Flight 583, cruising at an altitude of 30,000 feet. I stared out of my tiny window and began to mentally map my game plan for my return home. Call it the "Bad Brown Resilience," but sitting there amongst the clouds, I began to feel as indestructible as I had before so many unfortunate events had taken place in my world.

I said it once, and I'll say it again, without reservation.

I am a Brown. Around these parts, that name alone determines your destiny.

Some might say that I am, and always was, guilty by

association. I tend to believe that my only real crime was loving a man more than I loved myself. Whatever the case, I like to think that I brought a whole new meaning to the word BAD.

Maybe I give myself too much credit.

I don't know.

You be the judge.

ORDER FORM

Triple Crown Publications
PO Box 247378
Columbus, OH 43219
1-800-Book-Log

NAME	
ADDRESS	
CITY	
STATE	
ZIP	

	TITLES	PRICE
	A Hood Legend	$15.00
	A Hustler's Son	$15.00
	A Hustler's Wife	$15.00
	A Project Chick	$15.00
	Always A Queen	$15.00
	Amongst Thieves	$15.00
	Betrayed	$15.00
	Bitch	$15.00
	Bitch Reloaded	$15.00
	Black	$15.00
	Black and Ugly	$15.00
	Blinded	$15.00
	Buffie the Body 2009 Calendar	$20.00
	Cash Money	$15.00
	Chances	$15.00
	Chyna Black	$15.00
	Contagious	$15.00
	Crack Head	$15.00
	Cream	$15.00

SHIPPING/HANDLING
1-3 books $5.00
4-9 books $9.00
$1.95 for each add'l book

TOTAL $_____

FORMS OF ACCEPTED PAYMENTS:
Postage Stamps, Personal or Institutional Checks &
Money Orders.
All mail-in orders take 5-7 business days to be delivered.

ORDER FORM

Triple Crown Publications
PO Box 247378
Columbus, OH 43219
1-800-Book-Log

NAME
ADDRESS
CITY
STATE
ZIP

TITLES	PRICE
Cut Throat	$15.00
Dangerous	$15.00
Dime Piece	$15.00
Dirty Red **Hardcover**	$20.00
Dirty Red **Paperback**	$15.00
Dirty South	$15.00
Diva	$15.00
Dollar Bill	$15.00
Down Chick	$15.00
Flipside of The Game	$15.00
For the Strength of You	$15.00
Game Over	$15.00
Gangsta	$15.00
Grimey	$15.00
Grindin' **Hardcover**	$10.00
Hold U Down	$15.00
Hoodwinked	$15.00
How to Succeed in the Publishing Game	$20.00
In Cahootz	$15.00
Keisha	$15.00

SHIPPING/HANDLING
1-3 books $5.00
4-9 books $9.00
$1.95 for each add'l book

TOTAL $_____

FORMS OF ACCEPTED PAYMENTS:
Postage Stamps, Personal or Institutional Checks & Money Orders.
All mail-in orders take 5-7 business days to be delivered.

ORDER FORM

Triple Crown Publications

PO Box 247378

Columbus, OH 43219

1-800-Book-Log

NAME	
ADDRESS	
CITY	
STATE	
ZIP	

TITLES	PRICE
Larceny	$15.00
Let That Be the Reason	$15.00
Life	$15.00
Life's A Bitch	$15.00
Love & Loyalty	$15.00
Me & My Boyfriend	$15.00
Menage's Way	$15.00
Mina's Joint	$15.00
Mistress of the Game	$15.00
Queen	$15.00
Rage Times Fury	$15.00
Road Dawgz	$15.00
Sheisty	$15.00
Stacy	$15.00
Still Dirty *Hardcover	$20.00
Still Sheisty	$15.00
Street Love	$15.00
Sunshine & Rain	$15.00
The Bitch is Back	$15.00

SHIPPING/HANDLING

1-3 books $5.00

4-9 books $9.00

$1.95 for each add'l book

TOTAL $_____

FORMS OF ACCEPTED PAYMENTS:

Postage Stamps, Personal or Institutional Checks & Money Orders.

All mail-in orders take 5-7 business days to be delivered.

ORDER FORM

Triple Crown Publications
PO Box 247378
Columbus, OH 43219
1-800-Book-Log

NAME	
ADDRESS	
CITY	
STATE	
ZIP	

	TITLES	PRICE
	The Hood Rats	$15.00
	Betrayed	$15.00
	The Pink Palace	$15.00
	The Bitch is Back	$15.00
	Life's A Bitch	$15.00
	Still Dirty *Hardcover	$20.00
	Always A Queen	$15.00

SHIPPING/HANDLING
1-3 books $5.00
4-9 books $9.00
$1.95 for each add'l book

TOTAL $_____

FORMS OF ACCEPTED PAYMENTS:
Postage Stamps, Institutional Checks & Money
Orders, All mail in orders take 5-7 Business
days to be delivered